Once people die, they're not meant to wake up.

For college student Beck Murray, this doesn't quite sink in until he's sitting in a stranger's apartment, reading his own obituary. He has no memory of how he died or how he happened to wake up—all Beck knows is that he's been dead for six months, and now, incredibly, is not.

He assumes his biggest challenge will be explaining himself to his family and friends. This proves not to be the case as, one by one, Beck and his friends become the target of something evil. A darkness hangs over Beck, following every footstep he takes in his new life. He cannot fight it because he does not understand it. Soon, it becomes clear that Beck isn't the only person who's returned to life, and far from the only person in danger.

With the help of a young witch and a mysterious bookshop owner, Beck must learn to overcome the evil plaguing him before it drags him back down to the grave... and takes everyone he cares about with him.

THE COST OF LIVING

In the Darkness, Book Two

Emilie Lucadamo

A NineStar Press Publication

Published by NineStar Press
P.O. Box 91792,
Albuquerque, New Mexico, 87199 USA.
www.ninestarpress.com

The Cost of Living

Printed in the USA
First Edition
February, 2019

Print ISBN: 978-1-950412-27-3

Also available in eBook, ISBN: 978-1-950412-11-2

Warning: This book contains the death of a minor character and depictions of possession.

For Nicole—who could easily conquer the world if she tried, but has momentarily settled for conquering libraries…and who even had to edit her own dedication.

Chapter One

AFTER HIS FOURTH failed attempt to pull himself to his feet, Beck gives up and collapses against the pavement once more.

It's no use. He could have the willpower of Hercules, yet he wouldn't be able to haul himself off of the ground. His body is too strung out; his limbs are exhausted. He feels drained from head to toe. Whatever happened to lead him here, it sure did a number on him.

Here—where *is* here? Beck has no clue. Naked, in the middle of an unfamiliar street, with a dizzying headache and no memory of where he is or how he came to be there. That's where he is right now.

It's far from the best situation to be in. Not to mention the fact that the world's biggest storm cloud seems to be focusing all its wrath on him alone. Rain lashes his skin, chilling him, and the thunder booming overhead rattles in his bones. He tries to move once more, and a fiery pulse of pain shoots through his entire body.

Beck has had better nights.

He's wound up in some pretty undignified places over years spent growing up with his best friends, but this has to take the cake. This is a lot worse than the time his best friend James dared him to sleep on the roof in his underwear. This is even worse than the time he and his brother, Dylan got locked out of the house during a snowstorm and had to spend the night huddling for warmth on the porch. At least in those situations, he knew where he was. He had some choice in the matter, (even if it was between Dylan's bony elbow in his side or freezing to death). This—this is a whole new level of weird.

He tries to lift his head, and a pulse of pain sends it right back down again. Thunder crashes overhead, followed by a flash of lightning. Beck swallows past his parched throat, realizing for the first time what a dangerous situation he could be in.

"Oh man," he rasps, realizing too late that these are the first words he's said since waking up. This absurdity is not helped by the fact that he's scrambling around on his back like a lethargic bug. It seems like a miracle he's able to speak at all. "Mmm...c'mon, *c'mon...*"

It's no use. He can't pull himself to his feet. Defeated, Beck collapses back onto the pavement again and closes his eyes. He's so tired... Maybe a few moments' sleep will give him the energy he needs.

He's just about to drift away, when a sudden interruption startles him from his haze.

"You look like you could use some help."

The voice is deep, clear as a bell over the roaring storm around them. Beck jumps, eyes springing open. It would take more self-control than he possesses not to gape up at the shadowy figure towering above him, silhouetted against the distant glow of a streetlight.

He blinks up at the stranger in a daze, trying to make out any features past the rain and his blurry vision. The man looming above him is slender, not too tall and not too muscular. The fact that he seems unfazed at finding a naked guy in the middle of the street probably says the most about him. Being the naked guy in question, Beck's not about to judge.

Beck weighs his options. Common sense tells him not to trust shadowy figures in dark alleyways. Common sense also tells him not to pass out in the middle of the street naked, and not to wake up in the middle of a street with gravel digging into his back. Common sense is failing him today.

He isn't about to get up without assistance, anyway, so yeah, he probably could use some help. "Wow, you figured that out?" he croaks, and tries for a laugh. It comes out as a wheeze. Beck is left choking when he attempts to take in a breath. He collapses again onto the street, landing hard on his side. His chest convulses with each ragged cough. By the time he is able to breathe again, he's quaking like a leaf in a thunderstorm. Hell, that's just about what he *is*.

"Easy..." The figure is kneeling by his side now and has a hand on his back. He's warm; subconsciously, Beck leans into the touch. The smooth hand runs along the curve of his spine, leaving a trail of tingling heat in its wake. The pressure in Beck's lungs slowly ebbs away, like water receding after high tide.

"Feels like you've got a pretty bad fever," the man says, his strange, precise accent twisting the words until they sound more like a melody. "This rain can't be helping. Wanna get out of it?"

"Yeah..." Beck nods hazily. "That'd be real great."

Hands grip his biceps, helping him to his feet. Beck's legs feel like noodles. He stands up, wavers, and would have fallen back down were it not for the grounding presence keeping him upright. He tries to straighten up, and his stomach does a perilous somersault. Hot bile rushes up his throat, and he only has time to double to the side before he's heaving up acid.

By the time he straightens up again, he's trembling from the exertion. He feels dizzy enough that he's afraid to close his eyes, doubting his capability to open them again. When he tries to turn to his good Samaritan, he finds himself confronted with a sharp-featured face, dark eyes studying him and brows creased in concern.

"Sorry," Beck tries to say. It comes out garbled. Fortunately, the guy doesn't seem to care.

"Come on," he urges, hooking an arm around Beck's waist. "Let's get you someplace warm and dry."

Needless to say, Beck's in no state to argue. Besides, he isn't sure he wants to. The guy's being nicer than he has any obligation to be, and it's probably the fever talking, but his touch is the most soothing thing Beck can remember in a long time.

They don't walk far. The stranger leads a stumbling Beck down the street, and they pass only a few shops before coming upon one with its windows piled high with books. A sign above the door reads *Lehexe's Books* in spindly hand-painted lettering. The shop is dark enough that Beck can't make out much through the window, but Beck's new friend—Lehexe, presumably—doesn't hesitate to open the door. He hustles them both inside and shuts out the storm behind them. No sooner are they standing in the middle of the shop floor than Beck finds rain pooling at his feet, soaking into the wooden floor. He sways in an effort to keep from dripping, and nearly overbalances again.

Lehexe—busy fumbling with a set of keys near a door behind the counter—casts a look over his shoulder and huffs. "Try to keep upright for two seconds. You can do that."

Beck definitely can. He's not an infant. (If he maybe has to grab hold of the counter to keep his balance, well, he thinks the other man is too preoccupied to notice.)

The right key finally slips into the lock, and Lehexe opens a door to a darkened hallway. He turns to look at Beck, raising an eyebrow as he gestures to him. Beck lets go of the counter, takes a step forward, and gets blindsided by a head rush that sends him falling on his face.

Being naked on the floor of some poor guy's very nice bookshop is better than being naked on pavement in the middle of a storm...but only just. There's a lot more indignity to his situation now that Beck is actually trying to keep himself upright. He *can't*. It's not just his legs refusing to cooperate with him. His entire body feels sluggish, achy and weighed down. His veins feel like they've been pumped full of lead. His skull is throbbing, stuffed with cotton and running with all the efficiency of a dying engine.

"I'm really sorry about this," he manages to slur into the nice stranger's woodwork. "'S not my day."

"I figured," Lehexe says as he helps peel Beck off the ground—and he is *really* being much nicer than Beck deserves. "I hope stuff like this don't happen to you often."

"It really doesn't." This is the weirdest thing Beck can remember happening to him in, well, ever. He's not handling it well.

By some miracle, Lehexe manages to get him back on his feet again and leads him out of the shop. The hallway behind the door is small, narrow, with several doors lining the walls. One clearly reads *Bathroom*; the other, Beck suspects is a closet; as for the third, he doesn't have a clue what could be behind it. (His half-delirious mind flashes back to the vintage game shows his grandma used to love, where shoulder-pad-flaunting contestants chose between Door One, Door Two, and Door Three for the chance to win "the prize of a lifetime!" Lehexe doesn't make a good game show host, and Beck's hairstyle isn't nearly exciting enough for 80s television.)

There's a final door at the end of the hallway, styled differently from the others. This one is great mahogany, with a firm frame, and another lock just beneath the knob. Lehexe turns to his set of keys yet again, and in seconds he has the door open to a set of stairs that tower over Beck's head, making him feel dizzy.

His heart sinks. His stomach drops. He feels himself slump further to the floor, until Lehexe stubbornly hoists him back up again. Just looking up there makes his head spin, and the notion of dragging his noncooperative body up the stairs is nothing short of a pipe dream. There's no way he can do it—just no chance.

"Yeahhh," he groans. "Dude...don't think that's gonna happen..."

"You gotta try for me," Lehexe says. "Can you do that?"

Beck considers this. "If I pass out, will you catch me?"

"I'll try my best."

Well, that's good enough for him.

They're about a quarter of the way up the stairs (a big accomplishment, in his opinion) before Beck starts really feeling like he's going to wind up spread across Lehexe's stairs like an unconscious, human-sized welcome mat. The other man still has a vice grip on his arm, but that's all that's keeping Beck moving. As he struggles up one stair after another, his vision begins to black out.

"Hey, hey, stay with me," Lehexe says, shaking him back to consciousness again. Beck lets out a whimper, slumping over sideways, but Lehexe rights him before he can tumble down the stairs. It seems like the other man is determined to drag Beck up there by sheer force of will, and Beck thinks he could do it, too. "What's your name?"

"Mmm. My last name..." He can answer that much at least, even if focusing on anything is really difficult at the moment. "'S Murray."

"Great. You got a first name?"

He stumbles over the word a few times before he just gives up. Hauling himself up these stairs is draining too much energy, and it takes all of his effort to stay on his feet. There's a few seconds of silence—he almost forgets that Lehexe is here, forgets he's walking instead of climbing a mountain or swimming through a roiling sea—when he hears a huff of breath. "You're not light, Mr. Murray."

Beck's hand reaches out blindly and catches upon something solid. He isn't sure what he's holding until he feels a muscle flex under his grip. He must be holding a bicep, then. "Wow. Okay. Had no idea we were that friendly already," Lehexe remarks.

Beck makes the mistake of opening both eyes at the same time. Maybe that's his big mistake. One second Beck is standing upright, and the next second he's just too dizzy to stay up any longer.

He's so tired, and everything hurts. All he really wants to do is put his head down for a second—is that so bad? The stairs are a lot nicer than the street anyway, a lot drier and less cold, and Lehexe is here with his low voice and warm hands, prodding him, "*Get up, come on!*"...

It's not a bad idea, but Beck just can't do it right now.

He has a brief flash of guilt for passing out in the middle of Lehexe's stairs, as well as for how much trouble he knows his unconscious body will wind up being, but it's not enough to keep him awake. He slumps against his arm and is out cold before he even realizes he's laid his head down.

WHEN BECK REGAINS consciousness, things are a lot...softer.

He knows he's in a bed even before he opens his eyes to see the dark comforter engulfing his body. The mattress beneath him creaks when he moves, though the persistent heaviness in his limbs prevents him from doing much. He knows even before he remembers where he is that he will not be able to get out of bed. His head pulses with what feels like the worst hangover he can remember. His stomach is still churning, and his body aches like he's been crushed by a steamroller.

He is able to turn on his side, attention lured by the warm light shining from the corner of the room, and can't help but groan at the head rush this gives him. Even lying down he shouldn't be so dizzy—what's *wrong* with him?

His brain feels muddled, and he'd kind of like to go back to sleep again—but his mother's many lectures on being aware of your surroundings kick in, forcing him to try to take in his location. It's clear that he's in someone's bedroom; the room seems lived in, clothes hanging off the back of a chair and a desk messy with paperwork. There is a closet at the far end of the room, and a round window over Beck's head, giving him a front-row seat to the storm raging furiously outside. Every so often, lightning will flash, illuminating a bit more for Beck's roving curiosity to take in: several framed pictures hanging on the wall, a towering bookshelf at the far corner of the room, a laundry basket on the floor. The bedroom door is closed, but golden light streams in from beneath the doorframe, drawing Beck's hazy attention.

For a long moment, all he can hear is the storm. Then, in a brief lull in the rain, voices become audible from the next room over.

"Whatever is happening," an unfamiliar voice says, light and high in a way that denotes it as female, "is far more serious than that. Magic like this..." Beck furrows his brows as he struggles to make out the rest of the words, but her voice is soft and fades in and out of his hearing. "...nothing we've seen...a war below...could get involved...this boy...dangerous."

"You don't know that," another voice—Lehexe's voice, and Beck realizes with embarrassment that this has to be *his* room—says. "He seems harmless...needed help...sick..."

"...reeks of magic," the woman says. "...nothing you've heard of?"

There is a pause, as if Lehexe is hesitating (or maybe Beck just can't hear him). When he speaks again, he sounds reluctant. "Never seen...back to life...spells like that..."

"Could it be—" the woman says, and whatever follows Beck really doesn't get to hear. A crash of thunder booms overhead; he is ashamed to say he jumps, arms flailing out wildly. Something from Lehexe's night table hits the floor with a clatter.

That's all it takes to cut the voices off. Having given himself away, Beck sinks into the bed and waits for the inevitable. Sure enough, it's only a few seconds before Lehexe is sticking his head through the bedroom door.

"Mr. Murray," he says when he sees that Beck is awake and opens the door wider. "Glad to see you're up."

Beck hums, sluggish tongue struggling to form words. "Gotta say," he mutters, "this's the worst hangover I've had in a while... 'N it's not even mornin' yet..."

He's sure he sees something flicker in Lehexe's expression, but it's too dark for him to make out. The man moves toward the bed, and Beck realizes what he's got in his hand only when it is unceremoniously shoved under his tongue—a thermometer. He tries to make a noise of protest but is hushed with a roll of dark eyes.

"If you're well enough to talk, you can be quiet and hold still," Lehexe says. "Give it a minute."

Begrudgingly, Beck does as he says. It's only a minute before the thermometer beeps again, and Lehexe withdraws it with a frown. "One hundred and three," he declares, shaking his head. "We gotta get that fever down, Mr. Murray."

"Beck," he corrects before he realizes what he's saying. Lehexe quirks an eyebrow at him. "'S my name. First name. 'S what people call me."

Lehexe looks pensive. "Is that your real name?"

"Nah. 'S Thomas." Beck makes a face and feels victorious when he sees Lehexe crack a smile. "But nobody calls me that. Just my ma, when she's ticked off."

"It's a nice name."

"'S a horrible name. Like an old man." Beck's head lolls against his shoulder, and it feels too heavy to pick up again. He settles for studying Lehexe sideways; when the man adjusts the blankets around his shoulders, he can't help huffing out a soft laugh. It's been a while since he was looked after like this when he was sick. (Beck doesn't get sick much—he gets hangovers a lot, but his roommate James's usual method of "taking care" of Beck involves throwing aspirin bottles at him while he's lying on the bathroom floor and laughing when they hit him in the head.) This is nice. *His new friend* is nice, he can't help but think, and notices once again how good-looking the other man is. He's handsome, in a quiet way, with strong features that underscore deceptively gentle black eyes. His skin is a rich sepia, and dark hair is cut close to his head. Beck can read the exhaustion on his face and feels a pang of guilt for stealing his bed.

If Lehexe minds, he doesn't let on. "I'm gonna bring you something for the fever," he says. "You sit tight, okay?"

"Not goin' anywhere, man," Beck says, and means it. He doesn't think he could move if he tried.

It feels lonely without Lehexe in the room. He settles for closing his eyes and listening to anything his ears can pick up—from the rain pounding against the window to the soft voices that resume in the next room, too low for him to make out. He tries to follow the cadence of Lehexe's voice, the highs and lows of his accent; it soothes him like a lullaby, and he doesn't realize he's drifting back to sleep until he's startled by the door opening again.

"Sorry," Lehexe says, at Beck's deer-in-the-headlights expression. "I brought tea."

"Tea? For a fever? Ain't there...medicines, 'n stuff like that?"

"There are," Lehexe agrees, sitting down on the edge of the bed as he balances the teacup in his lap. It's a casual gesture, but it strikes Beck as comfortable, in a way that puts him at ease. Lehexe seems like he's used to taking care of people; any potential awkwardness isn't present. "But this will work just as well. Come on, drink up."

Beck obediently sips at the tea. Lehexe helps him sit up and watches him until he's downed the entire cup. The tea is neither cold nor scalding, just the right temperature, and leaves a faint tingling sensation in his mouth. It carries a heavy taste of herbs, mixed with just enough sweetness to make it tolerable. Only when the tea is gone does Lehexe nod and allow Beck to slump back against the pillows once more.

"I was gonna give you something else to help you sleep," he says, watching Beck melt back into the mattress. "But I don't think you'll need it."

Beck at least has the decency to feel guilty. "Sorry for takin' your bed."

"Nah, it's fine. Get some rest, Beck."

Beck pulls a face, making a soft noise of protest. "Hey," he says suddenly. "What's your name?"

Lehexe looks surprised. "Huh?"

"You gotta tell me your name. I told you mine. Fair's fair."

The man above him considers this for a moment before he smiles. He's got a nice smile, Beck decides; it melts away the underlying anxiousness of his face, making him look softer and more relaxed. "It's Adam," he says, low voice uttering the name like a secret. "Adam Lehexe."

"Adam," Beck tests out, halfway between wakefulness and sleep, and decides he likes the way it sounds on his tongue. "That's nice."

"Why, thank you." Adam laughs, a low sound that echoes over the rain. The mattress shifts beneath him. Beck's drooping eyes remain fixed on his shadowy figure, and he can't help but think this is a nice sight to doze off to.

"Night, Adam," he mutters, before his eyes close again.

BY THE NEXT morning, his head is clearer, and when he opens his eyes to the smell of something cooking, Beck is delighted to find that his stomach doesn't churn at the thought of food. He pulls himself from bed, wincing at the ache in his muscles that has not totally abated. His head still pulses, and some of the cloudiness over his brain lingers, but compared to last night he feels like a million bucks.

He's wearing clothes too, he realizes—a white T-shirt (which is a bit too tight) and loose shorts.

Oh God—is he wearing *Adam's* clothes?

Panic might spur him out of the bedroom, but the smell of breakfast definitely helps. He doesn't know what he was expecting, but somehow he's not surprised at all by what he spills out into—a cozy-looking living room with a wall-embedded countertop splitting it off from a small kitchen. One small door in the corner is ajar, leading to what looks like a bathroom. A row of windows against the far wall are guarded by heavy curtains, now drawn back to fill the apartment with sunlight.

A beige couch rests against the wall, facing a small television set that must have been bought at the turn of the last decade. Between them is a coffee table, messy with loose papers and dogearred books. There are several half-empty coffee mugs, their contents long since gone cold. Beck spots a remote buried halfway beneath the couch, hiding in the plush carpeting.

Most interesting, however, is the bouncy pop music filling the apartment, and the woman swaying to it as she scrubs the kitchen countertop.

"Um," says Beck, and the woman freezes. In the half second that passes before she's fumbling with her phone to shut the music off, a comical bolt of alarm flashes across her face.

"Did the music wake you up?" asks the woman in a softly accented voice, looking apologetic. Beck shakes his head slowly, trying not to seem like he's gaping around the apartment. The last thing he needs is to seem creepy, on top of everything else.

"Nah, I think it was more the...sleeping-for-twelve-hours thing."

"That will do it." She nods and picks up her handful of paper towels once again. "There's breakfast in the kitchen if you feel up to it. It should still be warm!"

He doesn't need to be told twice. Scrambled eggs and breakfast sausages are cooling in the pan, but they taste amazing to Beck. He'd gladly eat oven grease at this point.

Now that his stomach isn't turning itself inside out, it's desperate for food. He feels like he hasn't had a bite of food in months.

He's devoured the eggs and sausages to the last bite before it occurs to him that the woman might not have eaten. His eyes widen guiltily as he glances from the empty pan to where she's busy at the sink, but when she looks over at him, she smiles.

"Don't worry. They're all yours."

"Thanks," Beck says genuinely. When she passes him a glass of water, he accepts with a grateful murmur. Maybe drinking something nonalcoholic will help him get rid of this awful headache.

He slides into a seat at the kitchen counter, content to nurse his water in silence. The woman isn't as complacent. After a few seconds, she turns the music back on, softer than before, and begins to clean the counter again.

"Adam always tells me I'm more of a slob than he is," she says in a light voice, "but I don't believe it. He has mountains of books laying around and hasn't cleaned his kitchen since last year. I don't know how he can live this way."

"Well, he lives above his shop," Beck replies. The woman is clearly interested in making conversation and seems friendly enough. Beck's never been shy, anyways. "Maybe he spends more time down there than up here."

"You're probably right. Workaholic," she says, and then smiles. "Your name is Beck, isn't it? I'm Sophie."

"Good to meetcha." Beck offers a hand, realizing he's still clutching his glass, and pulls it back with a sheepish wince. Sophie's smile grows a bit broader.

"Where's Adam?" Beck asks, anything to distract her from his hopeless idiocy. Sophie turns towards the living room, shrugging her shoulders in a gesture that seems a bit too casual.

"He went out a few minutes ago. I asked him to do me a favor, but he'll be back soon, don't worry. He's been fussing over you since last night!"

No wonder—Beck stole his bed and probably ruined his entire evening. Adam didn't need some drunk, sick idiot passing out in front of his store. Beck has no clue why the hell he was so nice to him. "He asked me to bring you something to wear," Sophie adds (and *thank God* the clothes aren't Adam's). "I was surprised to get a phone call at midnight, especially when I heard what it was about."

Beck feels another pang of guilt and ducks his head to avoid meeting Sophie's eyes. At this point, he doubts he has much dignity left, but he doesn't want her to think he's stupid (despite the fact that he clearly is). Sophie is pretty, with ash-brown hair neatly tied back from her face with a blue scrunchie, and bright eyes set in a freckled, pleasant face. What's more, she's being much nicer than she has to be. Even if she doesn't live here—which, if Adam had to call her last night, she must not—he's still a stranger in her friend's (boyfriend's?) home. Not only has Sophie made him breakfast and found him clothes, now they're making small talk.

Beck feels embarrassed. He isn't sure what to do. A large part of him would be more comfortable leaving, but there's no way he can go without thanking Adam for everything he did for him. It's obvious Sophie is here to keep an eye on him, and he chafes under the idea of being babysat but reminds himself again he's in a stranger's house.

She must sense his unease, because Sophie gives him another smile.

"I made muffins," she adds, gesturing to a plate of chocolate chip pastries sitting in the center of the kitchen counter. "Do you like to bake?"

"I'm bad at it," Beck shrugs. "Never learned, I guess."

"Anyone can bake." Sophie waits patiently as Beck plucks a muffin off the plate. He blinks at it for a few seconds before popping it into his mouth, taking a large bite. An involuntary moan escapes him at the savory taste, and her grin widens.

"So," she says as she settles down at the counter across from him. She rests her chin in her hands, scrutinizing Beck with large cerulean eyes. "Are you a student?"

"Yup," he nods around a mouthful of muffin. "I'm a junior at Meacon. Studying poli-sci." Which is basically a responsible way of saying Beck has no clue what he wants to do with the rest of his life but needed to pick *something*. No doubt Sophie knows this as well, but she doesn't let on.

"I'm at Meacon too," she says. "I'm a senior!"

Sophie, it turns out, is from some small, French-speaking town Beck has never heard of up in Canada. She came to America to study after high school and is working on getting her medical degree. She's come to know Adam through a desperate need for medical textbooks, which he helped her obtain from his store at a discount. They've since become close friends, even if Adam has been out of school for several years.

To Beck's delight, Sophie is also familiar with his younger brother, Dylan. They're both medical students, even if Sophie is a few years ahead of him; they still share a class and compare notes after confusing lectures. They've even gotten lunch together once or twice, according to Sophie. Beck is left wracking his memory for any time his dorky little brother might have mentioned having lunch with a pretty girl with a French accent.

If he hasn't shared anything about Sophie with Beck, Dylan no doubt has mentioned her to Dana, or at least to James. It's rare that the four have many secrets. Being in each other's business is a consequence of sharing a house, as well as growing up in the same neighborhood for most of their lives.

Beck was born in Newark's largest hospital and placed in the nursery right next to James. Ever since then, they've been inseparable—the "terrible twins," as their parents used to say (even though stocky, Italian James has always stood in stark contrast to Beck's eyesore ginger hair and freckled face).

James started dating Dana in junior year of high school, and she quickly became another part of the team. When they both wound up getting accepted into the same school in the much smaller town of River Falls, Rhode Island, it was just common sense they'd all move together. (Everyone insists Beck's major isn't a real degree, but it's more realistic than James's criminal justice aspirations. Dana is either going to wind up managing a company or taking over the world.) When Beck's younger brother was accepted into Meacon University's prestigious medical program, he came down to join them. That's the way they ended up: Beck and Dylan, Dana and James.

Their life hasn't changed much since New Jersey—the only difference is they're in a smaller town now, and they don't have their families hanging onto their backs. Beck would be lying if he said they didn't take advantage of that. Some of the stuff they've gotten up to has been pretty wild— which is why he's mortified over what happened last night, but not that surprised.

He tells Sophie as much, through a blush that must dye his face bright red as his hair. "My friends and I have put each other up to so much wild stuff that I'm surprised any of us are still alive. Not that that's an excuse," he hastens to add. "What happened last night... Well, I dunno what the hell happened. I'll get outta your hair soon, promise. I just wanna thank Adam for being such a great guy. Then I'll get goin', but I need to thank him first."

He's sure he sees a flicker of something uncomfortable on Sophie's expressive face—just for a second, before her head spins towards the door. "I think you'll get your chance," she says over the sound of footsteps pounding up the stairs. "He's home."

Adam enters the apartment several seconds later, keys dangling from his hand. He takes in Sophie and Beck at the counter before offering a close-lipped smile. "Good to see you up," he says to Beck; before he can reply, another figure trails after Adam and shuts the door behind her.

The girl who follows Adam into the apartment is built like a bird: slender, with long, bony limbs and a small frame. She has dark hair, falling to her shoulders in loose waves, and tawny skin. Her eyes are trained on Adam until she enters the room and registers the other people. She takes in Beck first, gaze sharp and suspicious, before landing on Sophie. A small bit of tension fades from her shoulders.

"Alyssa!" Sophie stands up quickly, plastering on a bright smile. It's not the same one she was giving Beck while they were talking. This has a note of urgency to it, a little too forced to be real. It's the same one she gave Beck when he walked out of Adam's bedroom. Now that he's seen her real smile, he can tell the difference.

"How are you feeling?" she asks the younger girl. When Alyssa shrugs without a word, Sophie turns her wide eyes on Adam.

"She's looking good," he says with a shrug. "I'd give her a clean bill of health. No fever, no aches and pains... She's doing just fine."

"Fine," repeats Sophie, a hint of something Beck can't identify in her voice. She fixes an earnest look on Alyssa.

Alyssa offers her a faint smile in return. "Fine," she echoes in a low voice. Beck catches her eye for a quick second before she averts her gaze, turning away. He's not about to say it out loud, but something about Alyssa doesn't seem "fine" at all.

As Sophie starts to bustle over Alyssa, urging her to sit down in the kitchen, Adam turns his attention back to Beck. "How're you feelin'?" he asks, in that same low voice Beck remembers well from last night. Hearing it with a clear head, he finds that his feverish mind hadn't exaggerated at all. Adam has a voice that carries like a gong, deep and lyrical. It seems to fit him perfectly. Adam himself is serious, soothing, with an underlying air of something mysterious that Beck can't help but find a thrill in.

(Jesus, he's known the guy for less than a day. James was right—Beck does romanticize things too much and is weak for an attractive face. In the time he's known Adam, he's thrown up at his feet, made him carry his unconscious body up the stairs naked, and stolen his bed for a night. It's safe to say Beck has no chance, even if Adam *was* into men.)

"I'm feeling great," he says, forcing his brightest smile as he tries to smother every ounce of attraction he feels for the other man. "A lot better! The hangover ain't even that bad!"

"Hangover, huh?" Adam raises an eyebrow.

"I've had way worse!" Beck chirps, then shuts his mouth abruptly. Geez, he sounds like an alcoholic. Ignoring the urge to smack himself in the face, he instead crosses the room and offers Adam a hand.

"Hey, I just wanna thank you. For helping me out last night, ya know? It was great of you—I have no clue why you did it, but geez, thanks a lot. I know I've been a pain, so I'm gonna get out of your hair, but I just had to thank you. If I can give you anything—money, whatever—just name it. I have no idea what the hell was going on last night, but you were way nicer than I deserved."

Adam drops his hand awkwardly, shifting in place. Beck is surprised by how out of his element he suddenly looks. He hopes Adam doesn't think he's offering him charity money— he's doing better in the financial department than a mostly broke college kid anyway. Was offering cash too much? Just as anxiety is starting to grip Beck like a vice, Adam looks at him once again.

"Actually, Beck... I kinda wanted to talk to you about that."

Beck stands up a bit straighter. There's a look on Adam's face that he recognizes, and he doesn't like it. It's the same expression Mrs. Petrucello wore before she told them that James's brother had died in Afghanistan. It's the same expression Dylan wore when he learned he was failing three classes and at risk of losing his scholarship. It's the same expression Dana wore after one of her and James's worst breakups.

Something isn't right.

"Adam?" he asks, suddenly nervous. "What's the matter?"

Adam sits down at the counter again and gestures for Beck to do the same. He hesitates; Adam is waiting, Sophie is watching him, and even Alyssa pierces him with a dark-eyed gaze. Suddenly, anxiety roils in the pit of his stomach. His eyes flicker towards the door, and he wants more than anything to race out of that apartment.

Instead, he sits down across from Adam.

"What do you remember about last night?" Adam asks. Beck shrugs, mind automatically flickering back to waking up in the street. He recalls the thunder crashing over his head, icy rain pounding his skin. He recalls remembering what his grandmother told him once, that when it storms the angels are battling in Heaven.

That's all he remembers. No James dragging him out to the bar, no wild parties, no burn of alcohol in his throat. It's just...darkness.

"Not much," he confesses, and swallows hard. "I, um... I think I was drunk. Really drunk. And sick too, I guess, but my buddy's a doctor so I can't believe he didn't notice, he's usually on top of stuff like that—"

He cuts off his rambling with a click of teeth and looks up at Adam. He feels a little sick and wishes he knew why.

"Do you remember what was in the news last week?" Adam asks. His words are slow, careful. "About that bar that exploded. Some sort of gas leak?"

Beck draws a blank. Surely James would have been ranting about that. Hell, he probably would have gone down there and tried to help out. He shakes his head.

"What about that earthquake? It hit a cemetery hard, split a mausoleum right down the middle. You remember that, right?"

Beck shakes his head again. His chest feels tight.

Adam looks up and exchanges an unreadable glance with Sophie. Alyssa isn't looking at either of them; she is scowling down at her hands, shoulders barely rising with each breath. Adam turns back to Beck again, and anger flares suddenly in his chest.

"Adam, what the hell are you tellin' me?" he demands. "I'm a busy guy. Maybe I just wasn't paying attention. Is that so weird, huh? Why're you—"

Wordlessly, Adam slides his phone across the table.

Beck catches it before it can slide off, and frowns down at the webpage it is open to. At first he thinks it's a news article—it is dated a few days after January 1, New Year's Day. He knows instinctively this is recent (even though there are no holiday decorations around Adam's apartment, maybe he just cleans up early). Then he focuses on the picture at the top of the article and feels his heart stop.

It's his face—his bright eyes, his warm smile beaming beneath a headline that reads *In Loving Memory of Thomas Becker Murray (1995–2017)*.

For a long moment Beck doesn't move, staring with wide eyes at the article. It's your standard obituary: when he died, who he leaves behind, a few spare facts about him, and where services will be held. His whole life and death, boiled down to barely a paragraph. His grin mocks him from the top of the page.

"That...was two months ago," he breathes, pointing at the picture. It was taken at Dylan's last birthday party, in October. It had been a group shot—he, Dana, and Dylan, with James behind the camera. (*"Dylan, you ass, quit makin' that weird face! Okay, everybody look like you actually like Beck!"*)

Adam's brows are furrowed, expression closed off and unreadable. "Beck, this article was written in January. It's July now. You've been dead for seven months."

That's the moment Beck's world drops out from under him.

He can't speak. He can't breathe. The phone drops from his hands as if it's burned him, but he doesn't try to stand up. His mind is an out-of-control merry-go-round, whirling thoughts and emotions and desperate attempts to rationalize what he's just seen crowding his mind in a cacophony of chaos.

What? That's—no, that's impossible. He can't be dead. He's right here, he's alive, he can feel his heartbeat, he can't be dead—it's New Year's, it was *just New Year's*, he—

He doesn't remember New Year's.

He realizes with a sharp stab of alarm that he doesn't remember New Year's Eve. He doesn't remember waking up on the first day of the year. He doesn't remember partying with his friends, he doesn't remember calling his family, he doesn't remember—

He doesn't remember.

What happened last night? How could he wake up in the middle of the street, naked and sick as a dog? He'd assumed he was drunk, but why can't he remember drinking anything? Why can't he remember how he got there?

"No," he says, not recognizing the sound of his own voice. "I'm not—I'm not *dead*."

"I'm sorry, Beck," Adam says, and he really does sound apologetic. Like he's offering *condolences*. Beck feels sick.

He doesn't remember dying. Of all the things a guy could forget, that seems like a pretty big one. Yet somehow his obituary is sitting right in front of him, and bright summer sun is shining through the windows of the apartment. Half a year has passed without him realizing, because he's apparently been *dead*—

Until he woke up in the middle of the street last night.

Why the hell can he not remember?

Chapter Two

JUST THE FACT that Beck isn't hyperventilating is a miracle, but he's coming pretty damn close.

He's dead. He's dead, but he can feel his heart beating in his chest, can taste each breath of air, and hears his own panic ringing in his skull. How the hell can he be dead when he's alive?

It's impossible. Humans don't just come back from being dead. He couldn't have just *died.*

Everyone in the room is staring at him, watching him melt down before their eyes, but Beck doesn't care. How can they expect him not to freak out when he's just been told he's been dead, and he can't remember a thing? "I can't believe this," he blabbers, hands tangling in his short hair. "I can't, I freaking can't *believe* this. It's a joke. This has gotta be a goddamn joke, you can't be serious—"

"Beck, please calm down," Sophie says, but Beck rounds on her with wide eyes of disbelief.

"Calm down? I'm *dead*! I just read my own damn obituary! Why don't you try to calm down when you find out you're dead, you've *been* dead for seven months and have no clue what's going on—"

"Hey!" Adam exclaims, and it's this that finally snaps Beck out of it. His sharp tone severs through Beck's panic with the efficiency of a knife. It's such a contrast to Adam's usual controlled, calm tone that Beck's body freezes up before his mind can register it. Only when he turns to look at Adam does he realize the other man isn't angry but is fixing Beck with a very determined gaze.

Only once Adam sees he has Beck's attention does he speak again. "We're not freaking out, okay? That ain't gonna help anybody. We're gonna figure out what's going on here but freaking out will only make things worse. You've gotta keep it together, Beck."

"Keep it together?" Beck's voice is a disbelieving squeak. "I'm dead, Adam. And I don't even remember how I died! The hell am I supposed to 'keep it together'?"

"Well, you better figure it out, because there will be no flying into a blind rage in my house," Adam says, voice stern. Beck is reminded sharply of his mother, and how protective she is over her neat-as-a-pin dining room (with four kids, she had to defend that room like a warrior). He knows better than to test Adam on this—and maybe that's what finally gets him to sit back down.

Sitting does little for his nerves. He can still feel his heart pounding, fit to burst out of his chest, and his blood pulses in his ears. Even so, Adam trains a piercing dark-eyed gaze on him, and Beck finds it impossible to tear his eyes away. The longer he sits, staring back at him, the easier it becomes to breathe.

Only after a few long minutes does Adam break the tension of the room.

"I know this is a shock, Beck, but you've gotta understand what's been going on. A week ago, something went down in a cemetery a few blocks from here. It was just after someone broke into our shop and ransacked the place. We don't know who, and we don't know what, but we think a spell was performed with the intention of resurrecting the dead."

Beck inhales a ragged breath. "Resurr—you mean, someone tried to bring back dead people?"

"A dead person, yeah. Only, the spell used was made up on the spot—a combination of a bunch of different forms of necromancy all mixed into one ritual. Whatever effect it had was explosive. We don't know what happened to the person who tried to do the spell, but ever since then a lot of bad magic has been swirling around."

"Demonic," Sophie clarifies in a low voice. "There is a lot of demonic energy in the air."

"And ever since then people have started..." Adam trails off, throat bobbing as he swallows. "More than one person has woken up, when they shouldn't be. They're coming back. That's what's happened to you, Beck."

Oh God, this is three shades more crazy than Beck ever wants to deal with when he's got a headache. He shakes his head slowly, trying to dislodge the clutch of panic around his ribs on top of all the information refusing to sink into his head. "What—" he starts, then stops, laughs hysterically, then starts again. "So, no one tried to bring me back? I just woke up 'cause of a damn accident? Well, who the hell was supposed to come back?"

"We don't know," says Adam. "We don't know who the witch was, either. We don't know how many people are coming back. Far as we know there's been you, one or two other people in the newspapers, and—"

"I'm not alone, then." Beck seizes on this and pulls himself to his feet once more. "You mean, this is happening to other people too?"

"Beck, we're working to figure this out!" Sophie speaks up. She has one hand protectively clasping Alyssa's own where they sit together on the couch; she massages her thumb over the nervous-looking girl's knuckles. "We're going to discover exactly what's going on, but in the meantime you've got to work with us."

He reels back, shaking his head. He can't become the lab project of a few people who seem to know more about magic spells than any ordinary person should. If he's really been dead for months, then his friends... God, his *parents*...

"I can't stay here," he says. "I gotta go home."

Sophie opens her mouth, looking like she wants to argue. Adam sees the storm on the horizon and grabs the wheel before she can drive them straight into it. "We can't keep you here," he says. "You can go when you want, but Beck, don't you want to figure out what's going on here? You don't know how healthy you are, and if something happens—"

"I feel fine." He's not sorry for cutting Adam off. Suddenly, all of his thoughts are outside this apartment, on the doorstep of the house his friends have rented on the other side of the city, and back in the streets of Jersey, standing in the front yard of his childhood home. If he's cooped up inside here for another minute, he's sure he'll die all over again. He needs to find his people. He can't stay here with these strangers, trying to convince him that he's some freak of nature.

He just needs to get home, and it will all make sense.

"Sorry, Adam," he says, shaking his head at the man. "Sophie," he adds, turning to nod at her. He's slowly backing up towards the door. "I can't stay here. You've been nice, you get it, but I gotta—go—you understand." He feels breathless, a little hysterical. "I've gotta get home."

Sophie stands up, but Beck is already at the door. No one is about to stop him, and maybe Adam realizes that, because he doesn't even try. He just nods his head, a respectful if reluctant incline.

"Good luck, Beck," he says, and that's the last thing Beck hears before the apartment door slams shut behind him.

HIS STREET LOOKS exactly the same way he remembers it—rows of houses lining both sides of the road, in various states of disrepair. The same shutters are hanging from the same windows. The couple in the blue house still haven't repaired their broken porchlight; the mailbox that Dylan ran over last Halloween hasn't been fixed yet.

Even so, he cannot help but notice the differences. When he'd last stepped out of his front door, the world was painted in dingy, dull-colored hues of winter. Now every lawn is lush, green, and in many cases overgrown. The massive elm tree in their neighbors' yard no longer stands tall, a stump the only monument to its years of existence. There is a brand-new car in the driveway of the house at the end of the street.

With every step towards his own house, Beck can feel his heart pounding faster. This is the place he has come to call home over the past three years, yet somehow he feels like a stranger, an unwelcome intruder. This is his street, but it is not really his anymore.

He climbs the steps to the porch, rebelling in the familiar creak of wood. He knows every weak spot in those stairs, and that leaning on the railing will cause it to topple over. He knows the smashed porch light will still light up; he knows ringing the doorbell hasn't done anything for years. He remembers every inch of this place, his home. *His home.*

He belongs here, he tells himself as he pounds barefisted against the door. He belongs here.

(What if his friends don't welcome him back? What if they treat him like a freak, an impossibility? What if their reactions confirm what he desperately does not want to believe? What if—)

The door swings open.

"You gotta be fuckin' kidding me."

For all the things that have changed, Daniela Ramirez Scarrone is exactly how Beck remembers her last—confident, steely, and sharp as a knife. Chestnut curls frame a round face, dark eyes fixed on Beck that are half-disbelieving, half-amazed. She still barely stands as tall as Beck's shoulders, still with the same curvy figure and daring red lipstick. She has not lost the proud set to her shoulders, or the boldness that seeps from every pore. She's the same old Dana, and she's staring at Beck now like she's seen a ghost.

Dana has always been fearless. When Beck takes a step towards her and she steps back—that's the moment he knows something is very wrong.

"Dani," he says, and prays to God she isn't about to slam the door in his face. "It's me."

Dana's eyes look large in her pale face. The hand holding the door open trembles slightly. "Beck?"

"Yeah. Yeah, I'm here, it's—the weirdest shit has been happening, Dani, Jesus, I don't know what's going on—"

"What's going on?" Dana echoes and barks out a harsh laugh. "Are you kiddin' me? You're dead!"

"That's what they're tellin' me, but I can't be dead since I'm right freakin' here!" Beck doesn't mean to yell, but it's been a hard morning. His temper flares up, short and sharp, and he sees Dana's eyes go wide. Beck's has known her to be frightened maybe twice in all of the years he's known her, and this surpasses all of them. This isn't just fear—it's terror, desperate hope mixed in with disbelief, fury, and a little bit of despair. He's never seen that look on anyone's face before, and it sure doesn't belong on Dana's.

"I'm crazy," she mutters to herself. "Jesus Christ, you can't be here."

"Dani," Beck says, voice pitching up in a whine. "Please just let me in."

She stares at him for a long moment, deathly silent. Beck shifts under her gaze but forces himself to meet her eyes. She picks him apart, peeling away each layer of skin and unraveling every part she can get to for answers. When she reaches out a hand without warning, it's all he can do not to jump back. Instead he allows her to touch his cheek; their flesh connects, and she jumps back like he stung her.

"You're warm," she breathes. "God, you're real."

"I'm really here." Beck isn't sure if he wants to laugh or cry. "I'm not dead. I don't know what's going on, but I'm not dead. Okay?"

"Okay. Okay." Dana nods, her bob of curls bouncing, and takes a step back from the door. "Get in here; everybody's gotta see you."

Beck doesn't need to be told twice. He scrambles through the doorway, reveling in the sight of the familiar foyer. The rundown coat rack next to the door still stands proud, holding anything from umbrellas to swimming goggles, conspicuously bare of any actual coats. The "family pictures" that Dana and James took such care to hang along the walls leading upstairs are all in their places; so is the dubious looking carpet leading upstairs like the world's ugliest (red and brown checkered) runway. Everything is just as Beck remembers, and for a moment it's easy to forget he ever left in the first place.

It's good to be home, he thinks, and has to fight back a grin.

Then Dana brushes past him down the hallway, and he is dragged back to reality. He isn't home quite yet.

It's strange to be led through his own home like a visitor. Beck figures he should try talking as he follows Dana through the house, but he really doesn't know what to say. Dana must be facing a similar problem; in all the years he's known her, this is the first time Beck has seen her speechless. She keeps her posture stiff, eyes straight ahead as she leads Beck through the house all the way to the "studio."

The "studio" was dubbed as such through a collective vote, after Dylan insisted they needed an official name for at least one room in their house, just so they can pretend to be busy should anyone (i.e., their parents) call them. The "studio" is not a studio at all, and no work actually gets done there. It is a room with a leather couch, an ancient air hockey table, and the largest television in the house. This is where movie nights and video game showdowns happen, where snacks are eaten and the wildest food fights ensue. The very stern "no business in the studio" rule has been enforced since the day they moved in, and anyone who tries to bring house bills or homework into the room is summarily exiled to the backyard (no matter the weather; Beck's written essays in the snow more times than he cares to remember).

Beck loves the studio.

When he steps into the doorway, his eyes widen in relief. Of all the ways he'd expected to find his friends, the normalcy of the sight in front of him is a balm to his ragged nerves. Dylan is a familiar sight, lanky limbs splayed across the back of a chair, lying upside down with a game controller clenched in a white knuckled grip. He's running his mouth, the way he always does during a game, a stream of curses and unimaginative trash talk being drowned out by the screen's sound effects. James, at least, is capable of sitting like a human being. He might be lounging on the couch, but he is locked in iron-clad focus. They're playing a shooter game on the screen, one of the team ones that Beck has played before. Dylan is fighting against James and losing badly.

He can't help the wheezy laugh that escapes him, too soft for the room's occupants to hear. He opens his mouth to say something but is beaten to it.

When Dana speaks, she sounds tentative for the first time in her life. "Umm...guys?"

"Dani," James hollers, dipping his head back without tearing his eyes from the screen. "Get in here and help me kick this guy's ass!"

Dana swallows hard, throat bobbing, and takes a step into the room. "Turn off the game," she says over the artillery booms on screen and Dylan's continued cursing.

James still doesn't look up. "The hell ya talkin' about?"

"I said—" Dana says, voice pitching in frustration, but Beck beats her to the punch. He slips through the doorway, moving past her and snatching the last controller off the couch. "Mind if I play?" he asks.

Everything stops.

The game goes silent. Dylan's controller slips out of his hands, hitting the floor with a dull thud. James's fingers freeze over his own remote.

Slowly, his best friend turns his head to look behind him. "Beck," he says, very calmly, when he sees the figure standing there.

Dylan, still upside down in his chair, has gone stark white. Beck can't read his face, but he knows when his brother is freaking out, and he'd call that frozen expression a freak-out if he ever saw one. James is stone-faced. He doesn't even look like he's breathing.

"Hey guys," he says weakly. "It's been a while, huh?"

No one says a word for a moment that stretches on too long. The silence is broken by a shrill half laugh from Dana, who takes a step away from Beck while gripping the back of the couch like her life depends on it. She's inching towards James, who's got his square jaw set and is staring so hard at Beck that he probably doesn't see his girlfriend at all.

"What's goin' on?" asks James, finally shattering the awful silence that's fallen across the room. He isn't asking Beck—his tone of voice, like someone questioning a prank, makes it obvious—but Beck laughs and opens his mouth anyway.

"I dunno. I think you gotta tell me what's going on here, Jimmy," Beck says earnestly. "'Cause seems like I've been gone for more than half a freakin' year, and then this morning I've got a guy showing me my own obituary, tryin' to tell me I'm dead!"

James's eyes are very, very wide. He's got that mildly constipated look on his face, the one he always gets when he's trying hard to understand what the hell is going on but can't quite get it. "Well, yeah, Beck," he replies, slow and careful. "You *are* dead. At least, you're supposed to be..."

He knows it but hearing it from James is too much. James doesn't mess around; he doesn't waste his time with jokes that aren't funny, especially at his friends' expense. He would never lie to Beck like this. The fact that it's *James*, his friend since diapers and the person he trusts more than anything, looking him in the eyes and telling him he's *dead*...

The rickety, half-formed structures of Beck's world are crumbling around him, and he has no idea how to stop the decay. "What are you talking about?" he demands, voice starting to get shrill. His instincts are all haywire; they urge him a thousand directions at once, to pass out, or run out of the room, or jump out the freaking window just to get away from everyone in his life who've suddenly gone *crazy*.

Everyone can sense how on edge he is, because they instantly react the same way they've always reacted when Beck's upset. James stands up, holding up his hands in a placating gesture. Dana seems ready to lay a hand on Beck's arm, only holding herself back because she doesn't know how he'll react. It's just Dylan who still wears a look of horror; he's staring at his brother as if he's looking at a ghost. Oblivious to the stares of the rest of the room, Dylan is practically trembling. His dark freckles stand out against his stark-white skin; his eyes are huge and bulging. No matter how familiar the reactions of anyone else may be, Beck can't see anything but his brother.

"Take it easy," says Dana. "Why don't you sit down, Beck?"

"Sit down? You want me to *sit down*?" He feels hysterical, frantic. "Why don't you tell me what's goin' on, huh?"

"What do you remember?"

"*Remember*? I don't remember a thing!" He remembers this house, these people, he remembers his whole life; then he remembers waking up outside of Adam's shop. He doesn't remember the in-between, and sure as hell can't remember dying.

He feels his breaths grow ragged as they fight each other to escape his lungs. His head is spinning, blurring the world around him in a confused cacophony. He takes a stumbling step back from Dana's hand, and somehow trips over his own feet. When he goes crashing to the floor, James is instantly at his side and on his knees to help him.

"Okay," he says, in that low tone he adopts whenever he's taking charge. There is a pressure on both sides of Beck's face, anchoring him to the real world. It takes him a moment before he is able to focus enough to recognize it as James's calloused hands. He forces his chin up, dark eyes boring into his. For all the masked panic he's just seen from his friends, there is little of that in James's gaze. He looks in control, and that's the way James is *supposed* to look. Beck focuses on his best friend and feels himself breathe a little easier.

"We're going to figure out what's going on," James declares. "Let's all sit down, and we'll sort this the hell out."

THAT'S HOW BECK finds himself on the couch five minutes later, sandwiched between his friends. A heavy blanket has been wrapped around him, covering all but his face and hands. It leaves him warm and constricted, like being enveloped in a cocoon of pure safety. He nurses a steaming mug in his hands—when there's stress at home, Dana's first instinct is always to make hot chocolate, and Beck has never been more grateful for the tasty treat. He isn't sure whose presence is more soothing: James on his left, solid and steady, or Dana on his right, an arm wrapped around his shoulders with no plans of letting go anytime soon. Being surrounded by such comfort almost makes telling what he knows easy.

"...and that's when I freaked out. Because I couldn't believe it, ya know? Who wants to think they've been dead for half a year and had no clue about it? It's... I mean, it's not possible. But here I am. So I left there, and I came straight here, and hell if I have any clue what's going on right now."

Dana runs her hand up and down Beck's shoulder, and he can't help but lean into her. James's hand finds his back as well. His friend locks onto his shoulder, gripping like he never wants to let Beck go.

"This is nuts," James mutters, leaning forward. "Here I was thinkin' you were a ghost, or some idiot's idea of a screwed-up prank. But you ain't that, are ya?"

"I'm sure not," Beck says. The entire situation is so bizarre, and so screwed up, that Beck can't help it when he finds himself starting to laugh. "I'm so freaking alive," he giggles, "and I have no idea what the hell is going on!"

James snorts, caught up in the hysterics. Even Dana presses a hand to her face, releasing a few breathless half laughs as she shakes her head.

To be together with his friends again, and laughing, makes something inside of Beck warm up. He feels more alive than he has since the moment he woke up.

Then he sees Dylan.

His younger brother has still not moved from his chair, a safe distance away from everyone else. Now he is sitting up—back ramrod straight, shoulders tense, and face a hard mask that Beck can't read no matter how hard he tries.

Dylan isn't laughing.

This is so *wrong*, because Dylan is always the first to laugh. Hell, he takes pride in rarely, if ever, being serious. When nothing's going right, Dylan isn't about to fix anything, but you sure as hell can count on him trying to turn it into a joke.

It's because Dylan doesn't like serious things, and he hates seeing his friends upset. For him to look like that— horrified, uncomprehending, *disgusted*—sends a jolt of ice through Beck's core.

"Dyl," he says suddenly. His brother's dark eyes widen. "Come on, say something."

Put on the spot, Dylan doesn't seem to know what to do. He gapes like a fish, eyes flickering around the room for an ally. When he can find none, he turns back to Beck, defensive as a cornered animal.

"What am I supposed to say?" he demands, in a tone so harsh that it makes Beck cringe. "Yay, you're back from the freaking dead? Woohoo, throw a party! Beck's back, and everything's okay again!" He stares around the room, fury leaking into the incredulity that clouds his face. "How are you guys *acting* like this is all okay?"

"What the hell do you want us to do, Dylan?" demands James. "Toss him out on the street? Flip out, start throwing things and screaming zombies are finally here? Hell no. It's Beck. Our friend. However the hell he's here, he's here, and you can deal with it however you want."

Dylan does laugh now, incredulous and breathless. "Are you kiddin' me?" he spits. His voice is pitching higher, bordering just on the edge of cracking, the way it used to throughout all of puberty. When Dylan is flustered, he sounds like a twelve-year-old again. "You're just *okay* with this?"

"You're not?" demands Dana. "You of all people should be kissing Beck's feet right now."

"Did you forget what happened?" James adds, tone sharp. Beck hadn't realized it was possible, but the temperature in the room drops another ten degrees.

For a moment Dylan remains very, very still, eyes staring somewhere over their heads. He's not looking at anything; whatever he's seeing, it's nothing the others can witness. His jaw grinds, twitching slightly in the way it always does when he's trying not to explode. Beck has been caught in Dylan's explosions before—they're ugly, violent, and leave nothing undamaged. He opens his mouth to speak, but when Dylan sees this his eyes flash with fire.

"I'm *not* gonna freakin' deal with it," he declares, and storms out of the room before anyone can get a word in edgewise.

Beck stares after him, wide-eyed, until his brother disappears from view. The sound of the front door slamming echoes throughout the house. Once again, they are left in oppressive silence. The atmosphere in the room is heavy to the point of being suffocating. No one breaks the spell, because no one wants to admit that Dylan's reaction might have been the most logical out of all of them.

Beck is startled by a hand suddenly coming to rest on his knee. He looks over, pale and wary, to be met with Dana's face. The layers of foundation and mascara cannot mask the worry that knits the corners of her eyes; neither can they mask her intensity. Dana has always cared about everyone in her own way. She is passionately, painfully loving, and the determination that radiates from her eyes now causes Beck's breath to stall in his throat.

"It's okay," she says. "We may not have a clue what's goin' on, but we're gonna figure it out. All of us."

"Damn right," James agrees, and pulls Beck close to his chest. Beck is objectively larger than James, but when James decides someone is a teddy bear, they're a teddy bear whether they like it or not. He clutches Beck close, beefy arms wrapped around his shoulders, and barks out a laugh at the whine that escapes his prisoner. "You think you can get away from us that easily? Don't be stupid. It'll take more than dyin' before you're free from us!"

"Whatever's going on, we'll work it out together." When Dana says it, Beck can almost believe her.

In the embrace of his friends, with their support radiating from all sides, Beck finds it hard to breathe again—for a whole different reason. He couldn't ask for more from them, but being accepted with open arms leaves him feeling for the first time like everything might work out all right. He may have been gone for months, but everyone and everything is just how he remembers it.

(Everyone, he thinks ruefully, except for his own brother.)

BECK DOESN'T THINK he's ever been pampered this much in his life.

It's weird, having his normally boisterous relationship with his friends tossed on its head. Now, they alternate between acting like he's made of glass and treating him like a goddamn king. James, in particular, seems to have fallen victim to this. That familiar vein of overprotectiveness that verges on territorial has been nicked and is gushing strong; his big-brother mentality is out full force, with Beck on the receiving end. James is pushy about everything that evening, from having Beck change into his own clothes (his room remains mostly untouched—Beck can't be sure whether he's relieved or heartbroken at the fact) to trying to help him shower. Dinner is a chaotic affair, with Beck's plate being weighed down with more food than he could ever have the desire to eat. Trying to say "no" to anything just wins him a perfect copy of one of Mama Petrucello's famous scowls. Beck eats until he can barely get out of his seat, but James still tries to force more on him.

"If I eat another bite," he finally says, "I'll die all over again. Gimme a break."

In the face of Beck's fiery glare, James just grins like it's Christmas. "Hey, he's still got his old appetite!" he crows, clapping Beck on the back. "Good to have that mouth back, kid!"

Beck tries to keep frowning, but seeing the faces of his friends lit up around him makes his annoyance evaporate. There's no way for him to be cross. They've just got their friend back after having lost him. Of course they're going to be obsessed with him for a while. If he has to grin and bear it, that's what he'll do.

It's not all bad—James's cooking is still the best Italian food outside of his mother's own cooking.

After dinner is finished, they lounge around for a bit longer and chat. It's a callback to nights spent studying for exams, chattering away into the early hours of the morning and getting little actual work done. Beck falls into a familiar rhythm—bantering with James, then teaming up with Dana to take him on. For a while it's not hard to pretend things are normal.

(They don't talk about the past few months, and they don't acknowledge Dylan's absence. It's easy to ignore the unpleasant things, and Beck can't help but wonder if this was how they coped with *his* absence.)

It's a little past midnight when Dana announces her leave. "I've got class tomorrow. I've gotta get some rest."

Beck and James exchange skeptical glances, both aware she'll probably wind up working at her desk until early morning, but they're not about to stop her. It's been a long day, and surely Dana has as much to process as the rest of them. James pulls her in for one last kiss, and it lingers a bit too long for Beck's liking. Dana cups her boyfriend's face before pulling away.

(He and Dylan have both complained before about their friends' habit of showing their love in public. James just rolled his eyes and scoffed at them. "Someday the time's gonna come when we won't have each other anymore, and we'll wish we grabbed every kiss that we could.")

Dylan raised his eyebrows. Sentimentality has no effect on him; rather, he rebels against it. "And what about the day when you finally get sick of kissing each other?"

"That day will come long after we've gotten tired of looking at your ugly face," James had replied.)

Once she's gone, Beck finds himself alone with James. For a few moments it's obvious that neither of them knows what to say to each other. To find James speechless is a rare occurrence, but the silence stretches between them like a rubber band.

When James does speak, Beck isn't expecting it. The sudden "Beck" causes him to fumble with the penny he's been idly pushing around the table. It falls to the floor with a soft clatter but goes forgotten as he looks up into his friend's face.

James scoffs, rolling his eyes. "Quit lookin' like I'm gonna shoot ya. I have something I need to say."

Beck sits up a little straighter. "What's up?"

James pauses, hesitates, and runs a hand over his jaw before taking a deep breath. "It's good to have you back, you know? I mean...hell, it feels like a dream, like I'm gonna wake up in a minute and you'll be gone—we've all had that dream. But you're right here. You're...back." He aims a punch at Beck's shoulder. It connects, but there is no force behind it. "You ever do something stupid like die again, kid, and I'll kill you myself. But...it's damn good to have you back."

It's striking to see tears gleaming unshed in James's eyes. James never cries. He's easily led by his emotions and can be impulsive and rash at the worst times, but crying in front of others is something he doesn't let himself do. Beck has only seen him break down once, a week after his brother died.

James cried for *him*. The realization is like a stab in the gut, dragging him forcefully back to reality. He has to force a smile onto his face.

"I'm glad to be back, buddy," he says, laying a hand on his friend's shoulder. A small pulse of pain radiates through his head but compared to earlier it's barely a ripple. He pushes the discomfort away, allowing it to be drowned out in the tumult of his thoughts.

They linger for a while after that, but eventually the day's weight on James becomes obvious. After the third yawn smothered into his palm, Beck is the one to suggest that his friend head up to bed.

James is characteristically reluctant to go. "You wish. I'm not leavin' you down here alone."

"If I let you do that, you'll never leave me alone again." Beck huffs, though he understands his friend's concern. It isn't like he has plans to go anywhere else, or any other place to go. James knows that as well as he does. "I'm not gonna get into any trouble just before bed," he promises, waving him off. "Go on, it's almost midnight. Get to sleep."

It takes James a moment before the stubbornness fades out of his shoulders.

"All right," he agrees. "See ya in the morning, kid."

"Yeah." Beck smiles after his friend. "See ya."

Being left alone is almost a relief. It gives Beck time to think; time to digest the day, and how quickly his life has been flipped on its head. It's funny that something so massive could have occurred, and he can still go about living as normal. Home with his friends around him, it's easy to pretend nothing has changed at all.

Of course, that's not true, and he can't ignore reality. The fact is, something so massive has happened that no one knows how to digest it yet. Beck is trying to keep his head above the water, and his friends are the same way.

It's not long before being alone with his thoughts gets to be too much. He gets to work, out of desperation for something to keep his mind occupied. The remnants of their dinner from earlier in the evening have gone untouched. Beck busies himself clearing the table, throwing silverware in the sink and wrapping up what food remains unfinished.

Just as Beck is placing the last of the leftovers in the fridge, he hears the front door slam. Surprised, he closes the refrigerator just in time to see Dylan stumble into the kitchen.

His lanky form is swaying, eyes bright and face lined with sweat. He also reeks like the back room of a liquor store. Dylan's not old enough to drink yet, but Beck can recognize the smell of whiskey any day. It doesn't take a genius to realize his kid brother is dead drunk.

"Jesus, Dylan," Beck says, taking a step forward. Dark eyes fall on him, and Dylan's drunken swagger stops dead in his tracks. It only takes a minute of staring before his face twists up into a scowl.

"Great," he mutters, "you're still here."

"What's that supposed to mean?"

In lieu of an answer, Dylan turns on his heel and begins to stagger out of the kitchen. Not about to have that, Beck catches him by the shoulder before he can escape. He is unprepared for the violence with which Dylan whips around, eyes blazing with anger. "Don't touch me!" he spits, words smacking Beck in the face like a physical blow. Dylan jerks out of his grasp, and he reels back, stunned.

"I just—" he fumbles, at a loss. Shock and hurt sear his insides in equal measure, but in the end all Beck can come out with is an incredulous "What's your problem?"

"You wanna know my problem? Huh?" Dylan's words are slurred, but his tone is clear—seething and furious. He gives a wet laugh that catches in his throat, twisting it into what sounds like a sob. "My dead brother's standing in front of me. *That's* my problem, Beck. It's you."

Beck stumbles over his own feet, stung. He'd expected the answer, but that doesn't make it hurt any less. The fury on Dylan's face is seething, venom dripping from each word. This is more than Dylan's rash temper flaring up; this is pure *hatred*, something Beck's never seen Dylan direct at anyone, let alone *him*.

Every cell in his body wants to reach out to him, to demand that Dylan sit down and talk, but he holds himself back. He's worried that if he tries, Dylan might actually try to hit him. Plus, he isn't sure he could stand his brother rejecting him again.

Dylan draws himself up with all the dignity he can muster in his state, taking a step back. "Stay away. I don't wanna be involved in whatever shit this is, so keep it away from me."

With that, he's gone before Beck can get a word in edgewise. He's left staring at his brother's stumbling form, knowing that any attempt to follow will only make things worse. Beck is powerless tonight—he can do nothing but let Dylan walk away, no matter how it makes his stomach curdle.

"Dylan..." he mutters, but the name goes unheard. Beck is left alone, once again, with his thoughts.

HE THINKS THAT out of all the places in the house, the backyard will offer some solitude. He is wrong. He slips out into the warm night air to find the outside lights already on, illuminating the night in synthetic brightness. At the edge of the pool sits Dana, hunched forward with her elbows braced on her knees. Her nightgown is hiked up to keep it out of the water, red fabric spread out on the ground around her. Dark curls hang in her eyes, framing her round face and pensive stare. Her bare feet dangle lazily in the cool waters, filling the air with the sound of gentle splashing.

He feels bad for disturbing someone else and is about to turn back inside when she lifts her head. Her dark eyes fall on him, and, though she doesn't smile, she lifts a hand in greeting. "Hey."

"Hey," Beck echoes, wandering over to join her at the pool's edge. He lowers himself down to the concrete, surveying the water that stretches before him. Dana doesn't say anything more. He wonders what she could be thinking about, all alone out here at night.

He hangs his head, dipping his feet in the pool. It's unheated, chilling his bare skin, but the shock of cold is a relief. "I saw Dylan just now," he remarks. "He came home."

Dana picks her head up, eyes sharp with interest. Beck catches the flicker of relief that crosses her face. "He did, huh?"

"Yeah. Wasn't in the best mood." He knows his face has to give away how nasty the exchange was, even if his words are subtle. Dana heaves a heavy sigh, water rippling as she shifts her feet in the shallows. "I thought you were getting some sleep?"

"Well, I gave it a try. My head's too loud tonight. Too much to think about."

The thought occurs to him without warning that Dana really might not want him here, intruding on her peace. Maybe he isn't welcome out here—hell, maybe he isn't welcome here at all. Dylan clearly doesn't want to be anywhere near him, and even all of James's protectiveness and Dana's reassurances can't soothe the anxiety brewing in the pit of his stomach. If he doesn't belong here, he doesn't know where he should be.

"Is it wrong," he asks suddenly, "for me to be here?"

It takes Dana a long moment to answer. "No," she finally says, voice low with thought. "Of course not. This is your home. You belong here."

Her words help fill a bit of the hollow that has clawed its way through Beck's chest. The gnawing emptiness is soothed but does not vanish entirely. The memory of his brother's dark eyes still stings, and even thinking of them causes him to cringe in on himself.

He can see his own reflection in the clear pool water. He needs a haircut—ginger bangs hang almost in his eyes, scruffy and uncombed. His face might be thinner than he remembers, and his freckles stand out against his pale skin more prominently, but he's still himself. Nothing about him has changed drastically, aside from the fact that he's not supposed to be alive.

He's still himself. He's still *Beck*.

"It's just weird, you know?" Dana continues. "A little scary. After you died...it hit everyone real hard. Beck, you were cremated, for crissakes!"

Beck frowns. "Wait, you got me cremated? You burned me?"

"Well, you didn't exactly leave instructions." Dana casts him a side-eye, and Beck holds her gaze for all of five seconds before he's forced to look away. He breathes out, not sure whether he wants to laugh or groan.

"Did you scatter my ashes someplace cool, at least?"

"No. We lost 'em in the mail."

The worst part is, he can't tell if Dana is joking or not. He watches her lean forward, elbows against her knees, and run a hand through her short hair.

"God, I wasn't sure how Jimmy was gonna make it through. I've never seen anything wreck him so much, even after his brother died... For a while it felt like I lost him too. Your mom calls us every week, just to make sure we're all doing okay, but she's hurt even worse than we are. And Dylan... Beck, Dylan still isn't over you. It was the worst for him out of all of us, and losing you only to get you back... He just don't know what to make of it. None of us do, but we're tryin'. What else can we do?" She gives a soft, crackly laugh. "You're our friend. We've got your back."

He swallows, watching his reflection's throat bob. "That means a lot, Dana."

"Don't be like that. Don't act like you don't already know it. You'd do the same for any of us and more."

It's true. They're a family—it's the way they've always been. These are his people, and Beck is loyal to his people. If he had to, he'd die all over again for them.

"You're really not scared of me?" he dares to ask, and Dana huffs another laugh.

"Scared of you? Beck, you kiddin' me? I could take you down one-handed, we both know that. You can't beat Jimmy at arm wrestling, and even Dylan can probably knock your scrawny ass over. You want us to be scared of you, you're gonna have to try harder than this."

The answer is so typically *Dana*, and so reassuring that Beck can't help but smile. His reflection beams back at him, teeth gleaming, and he can't help but muse that he looks young. Younger than he feels, anyway—but maybe death really does age a guy.

"I don't know what you want to hear, Beck," Dana continues, "but as long as we're around, everything's gonna be—"

Her words cut off with a large splash, and Beck's reflection vanishes into the chaos of churning water.

In the split second that passes before he is on his feet, he has time to register three things: Dana is in the water; she is thrashing, hollering in surprise; and someone is holding her down.

Without stopping to think, Beck lunges. He slams into what seems like a solid wall of brick, bouncing off the side of Dana's attacker. Unfazed, he rears back and throws himself forward again, only to be met with a fist to the jaw. The blow takes him by surprise; Beck goes down hard but is already struggling to get up again when a fist buries itself in his hair and slams his head into the concrete.

His vision explodes into an incoherent blur of color. Sirens wail in his ears. It takes him a minute to realize this is not just ringing in his head, but Dana's screaming. This is what drives him to push himself up again, despite the pulse of pain reverberating through his skull.

Narrowed eyes lock on Dana's attacker as he tries to force himself to his feet again. It takes a moment for his vision to clear; when it does, he feels his heart stop.

The figure over Dana is unmistakable, down to the stocky build and lightly stubbled jaw. His face is twisted into a mask of rage, and his eyes are so dark that Beck can find no light in them, but there is no mistaking his best friend.

A strangled scream tears from Dana's throat but is cut off by a gurgle as James forces her under the crystalline water once more. Spray hits Beck's face from the force of her thrashing. She struggles against her boyfriend's iron-clad grip with every ounce of her strength. Dana isn't going under without a fight. She kicks, splashes, and howls even when submerged beneath the waves.

Beck forces himself to get up, ignoring the pain that radiates from his head. Dizziness blurs the edges of his vision, but he pushes past it. All he can focus on is Dana, drowning at the hands of her boyfriend. Dana, underwater and fighting for her life. James, holding her down, face set in a mask of unimaginable rage and eyes clouded pitch black.

Black eyes?

He tries to force himself to move to Dana's aid, but his mind is numb and his limbs have turned to stone. There is a steady ache in his skull, a pulse of static that, if he focuses on it, almost drowns out Dana's screams. What the hell is happening? Why can't he get up? Why is he frozen in place, watching his friend *die*?

(*He's seen this before. This is how it's supposed to be. He's been here before.*)

Dana surfaces, just long enough to gasp a lungful of air. Her fist swings up, connecting with James's jaw. James doesn't even flinch, simply recovering his grip on her shoulders. A second before she is forced beneath the waves again, Dana is able to gasp out a frantic "*Beck!*"

The shout echoes in Beck's head. A shield of glass shatters; a rubber band snaps. Suddenly he can breathe again, he can think again, and the spell paralyzing him is broken.

James doesn't get a chance to react before Beck slams into him, the full force of his tackle knocking them both into the water. Beck doesn't go under. He manages to find his feet, swinging back before either of them have a real chance to recover. His fist slams into his friend's jaw, and two hundred pounds of fury-wild James plunge backwards into the water.

Not a second later, Dana's head breaks the surface. Her labored gasps echo over the struggle behind her, and Beck's first instinct is to make sure she's all right. He doesn't get the chance before James is back, pulling him down. Now he's the one in over his head. There's no chance to escape, no hope of wiggling free...but Dana moves faster than a shot. Out of nowhere, she throws herself into the fray, leaping onto James's back and forcing him down as Beck struggles in James's iron grip.

James is still thrashing, the rage of a wild animal driving his movements. He arches his back to toss Dana off, a garbled roar tearing from his throat. Beck is abandoned; a cacophony of static wails in his ears as he surfaces for air. Dana is still on top of James, and Beck is quick to join her. Together, he and Dana are able to force James beneath the water's surface.

He's only under for a second. The second James's head breaks above the water, Beck decks him.

He goes down like a sack of bricks, falling back in a hail of water droplets. He would have slipped beneath the waves, but Dana seizes him around the waist, forcing him up. With Beck's help, they are able to tow James to the side of the pool and haul him out of the water.

By the time Beck has scrambled out of the pool, Dana is already crouched on the concrete. Soaked hair, hands wild on her face; her breaths come ragged as she fights off a rush of panic. She muffles curses into the hand pressed over her mouth, but her eyes are wide and fixed on her unmoving boyfriend.

"That's not him," Beck gasps. "That's *not* James!"

"No shit," Dana hollers back. "Who the hell is it?"

"I don't know, I don't know!" None of this makes sense. Nothing makes sense. James, the most loyal of them all, attacking his friends? It's *insane*. This could never happen—just like Beck could never have come back from the dead.

His mind flashes back to Adam and Sophie's words from earlier. *Spells...bad magic...demons...*

"Oh, Jesus," he hisses, and shakes James by the shoulders. He remains limp and unresponsive. If only he would wake up, open *normal* eyes so they could all know he was all right... "Jimmy, buddy, come on, come on..."

"Why the hell would he do that?" Dana's voice is shrill. "What the hell is wrong with him, what *was* that—"

"I think—God, Dani, I think he's possessed!"

"Well, what do we do?"

"I don't know!" Panic starts to clog his throat. This is so beyond any crisis he's ever dealt with before. He's surpassed his craziness limit for the day, and this is too much. He doesn't know what to do... He doesn't know anything about this...

But he knows someone who does.

"Dani," he gasps, "we gotta go. We have to take him to someone who can help."

Dana looks incredulous, and more than pissed off. She looks livid. Beck wouldn't want to be James when he wakes up, possessed or not. "And who the hell would that be?" she demands, arms locked around her own shoulders in a protective vice.

Beck swallows hard and draws himself up with all the calm he can muster. "We've gotta go to a bookshop."

Chapter Three

"BECK?"

Adam looks remarkably unruffled for a man answering his door at well past two in the morning. Wearing little else but boxers and a loose T-shirt, he lists against the entrance to his shop, peering with a furrowed brow at his unexpected guests. This is the second night in a row Beck has disturbed him, and he *really* feels awful about it.

Until he notices the black-rimmed reading glasses perched on the bridge of Adam's nose, and promptly decides that coming here was the *best decision ever*. Some people can't pull off glasses; Adam Lehexe is not one of these people.

(You're a weak man, Beck, a voice in his head that sounds a lot like James echoes in his head. He smothers it.)

Adam opens the door a bit wider. "What's going on?"

Flashing him what he hopes is more of a smile than a grimace, Beck holds up a roll of masking tape and gestures to the pickup stalled in the street right behind him. "Adam, I'm super sorry to do this, but we've got our buddy tied up in the back of our truck, and we're in a no-parking zone. You mind letting us in?"

Once again, Adam is way nicer than he has any need to be. Beck refuses to let him help as he and Dana haul the unconscious James out of the back of James's pickup truck. Adam is already opening his doors to them at an ungodly hour. The least they can do is handle their own dead weight.

Only once the two have dragged James up the stairs to Adam's apartment does Dana go back to the car. She returns leading along a stumbling Dylan, who's still half-drunk and more asleep than awake. Adam stares after their odd procession, bemusement clear on his tired face.

By some miracle, they all make it upstairs in one piece. Beck isn't sure how at least one person doesn't fall down—he nearly loses his footing once or twice—but he never thought he'd be so relieved to be back in Adam's apartment.

As soon as he closes the door behind them, Adam slips into a professional mode that Beck hadn't expected from him, but somehow isn't surprised by at all. Adam has already proven himself capable of taking charge during a crisis. "All right," he says, gesturing to Dylan first. "You can settle down on the couch and sleep it off. Let's get your unconscious friend into the bedroom—and really, rope? Untie his hands, for God's sake! What is he, an animal?"

"That's the thing, Adam," says Beck, biting his lip. "We don't know what he is."

Adam stares at him for a long moment, intense gaze piercing him. Beck is close to faltering under the stare when the sound of Dylan flopping down on the couch shatters the tension that has risen between them. Adam's attention turns to the drunk boy, then the possibly-possessed person on his living room floor. A long-suffering sigh heaves from deep within his chest.

"All right," he says. "You've all got some explaining to do."

THEY ONLY AGREE to allow Adam to call in reinforcements once he has made it extremely clear that he is not equipped to handle whatever they might be dealing with.

"Sounds to me like you've got a demonic possession," Adam says. (He doesn't look fazed. Does anything ever faze Adam, or is this just an ordinary week for him?) "You'll need an exorcism, and I don't do exorcisms. Ideally you'd want an exorcist, but I've got someone just as good who I can give a call."

Beck is the most reluctant of all, especially after he finds out Adam wouldn't be calling Sophie. James isn't crazy about the idea of bringing strangers into their business in general, and Dana wants to know why they couldn't do the exorcism themselves. Adam rebukes each of their concerns in a patient, albeit exhausted fashion: Sophie doesn't perform exorcisms either, and an untrained person should never attempt an exorcism, because there's a good chance of something going horribly wrong. This stranger is trustworthy, reliable, and experienced with possessions. He's their best bet.

Beck and Dane convene amongst themselves for a few moments, locked in debate. Bringing James to Adam was one thing, since Adam saved Beck's ass, which automatically counted him as trustworthy. This is different. The last thing any of them want is some stranger coming in and hurting their friend, maybe even killing him ("*I've seen those* Exorcist *movies, I know how this shit ends! I'm not about to watch my boyfriend try to fling himself outta windows or start spewing green shit.*") On the other hand, they have no choice. This stranger is their only option, and this is James—they have to do what's best for him. Beck takes one look at the faces surrounding him and realizes that Dana and Dylan aren't about to lose someone else they care about.

Dana speaks for everyone when they turn back to Adam once again. "Does your buddy do night calls?"

While Adam steps out into the stairwell to make the phone call, Beck helps tuck the still-unconscious James into bed. Being back in Adam's room is different now that he's no longer in bed himself. He feels almost like an intruder—as if he's getting a glimpse into some private part of Adam's life, even though he was here less than twenty-four hours ago.

"Jesus, Beck," Dana mutters, rolling James onto his back. "How hard did you hit 'im?"

James has been out for hours. He's got a hard head, and Beck knows his punch wasn't nearly hard enough to knock him out for this long. All he can do is shrug helplessly, frowning as Dana pulls the covers up to her boyfriend's chin. They peer down at his placid face for a moment before inhaling a collective breath. This tension is something they share, passed around like a bottle of bitter alcohol. They cannot escape it, no more than they can escape the reality of their friend lying in front of them.

Beck sees something pained flash over Dana's face—just for a split second, and then it's gone. He knows what she's thinking. He remembers how James was after his brother's death; for so long, he forced himself to remain stolid, until the moment he couldn't anymore. When he broke down, Beck and Dana were the ones who were there for him. After losing Beck...the thought that James had to suffer through that twice, and Beck wasn't there to comfort him the last time twists something in his gut.

Now it's James who's on the line, and Dana—who's always been strong for all of them—is facing down the loss of another person she loves.

Like hell is he going to let his friends go through that again.

"Come on," he says, jolting Dana out of her reverie. "Standin' here's not gonna help anything."

It's a relief to be out of that room, and he feels guilty to admit it.

CASSANDRA CARLYLE WALKS into Adam's apartment a little after five in the morning, looking tired, expectant, and a little annoyed.

"Lehexe," she greets Adam, "you owe me a huge favor after this."

"Nah," replies Adam, a tantalizing smirk decorating his lips, "you've owed me some favors for a while. Consider this you paying 'em off."

Whatever Beck had been expecting from Adam's friendly neighborhood exorcist, Cassandra...isn't it. She is small-figured and bony, but her fragile exterior is only highlighted by the brightly colored clothing she wears. Her sweater is oversized, hanging off her shoulder in a bright flower print; her jeans pool round her ankles. Cassandra has a thin face, sandy hair pulled into a messy ponytail on top of her head. The expression on her face is tolerant, as patient as possible for this time of night. Earthy brown eyes scan the room, falling on the cluster of people on Adam's couch, before Cassandra offers a close-lipped smile. "Good morning."

Beck takes in the newcomer, expression giving nothing away. "You the exorcist who's gonna take care of our friend?"

"I'm going to do my best," replies Cassandra, looking like she's just remembered a joke and is finding it funny all over again. Then her eyes flicker towards the bedroom. There is a sudden shift in her demeanor. She becomes more alert, holds herself a little straighter, looks more intense.

Adam doesn't miss it either. His eyes are sharp as he studies Cassandra. Beck is able to catch his gaze for one second and feels burned by the intensity there. Adam, he supposes, really is that way around everyone.

"Well, you've got something," mutters Cassandra, pressing her lips into a thin line. "Thanks for calling me, Adam."

Adam accepts this remark with a nod of his head, looking solemn. He breezes through cursory introductions more out of convention than anything else. "Cassie, this is Beck and Dana. Dylan's passed out next to 'em, but he's fine, just hungover."

"Yes! You mentioned that earlier!" Cassandra digs deep into the patchwork bag slung over her shoulder. It only takes a few seconds of rummaging around before she emerges with a water bottle, half-filled with bright orange liquid. The sight of it is enough to give Beck a headache. No drink outside of soda should ever be that color, and he has a feeling Cassandra isn't carting around Gatorade.

She sets the bottle on top of the mess of papers that is Adam's coffee table and nods to herself. "If he wants to spare himself some suffering, he'll drink that as soon as he wakes up."

Beck eyes the drink dubiously. It looks toxic. Dylan is far from a picky eater, but he's sure his brother would rather spend the morning burying his head in the toilet than put *that* in his body.

As if nature itself is in agreement with him, the bottle suddenly begins to wobble. It vibrates in place for a few seconds before tipping over. Nothing spills thanks to a tightly sealed cap, but the bottle rolls onto the carpeted floor.

"What the hell was that?" exclaims Beck, gaping at the overturned water bottle. Cassandra, rather than appearing startled, just sighs.

"*That's* a human spirit, but he'll act like a poltergeist any chance he gets. He's harmless, so don't be afraid of him. The worst he'll do is prank you or knock your stuff over." At Adam's questioning look, Cassandra shrugs. "He's been following me around for about a week now. He won't tell me much about himself, but he sure likes to talk."

"He got a name?" asks Adam, eyes flickering around the room. "You know I don't like spirits in my house."

"You need to refresh your wards, then," Cassandra replies gamely. She claps her hands together, drawing herself up after placing the bottle back on the table. It remains still—as if it had never moved at all, and certainly not on its own. Appeased, Cassandra turns towards the bedroom again. "Especially if you've got a demon in your bed. George, stay out here and don't cause trouble. Let's see what we've got."

Cassandra trails Adam into the room, leaving the rest of the group staring after them. Beck half rises, ready to follow, but Dana puts a hand on his arm to stop him.

"Give them a minute," she says, sounding like she doesn't like it any more than Beck does. "We're trusting them. Might as well go all the way."

"Adam says she knows what she's doing," Beck mutters as he returns to his seat again. "I wanna believe he's right."

They wait in silence, ears straining for any noise coming from the room. The room seems muted, as if someone has plugged their ears with cotton. In a small apartment, it shouldn't be possible for anything said in one room not to drift out to the next, but Beck can't make out a single noise from behind Adam's closed door. His bitten nails dig into his palms, and he can't help bouncing his leg. Dana shoots him a sharp look, but Beck can see she's grinding her teeth again, so she has no room to talk.

The silence is finally shattered by a low groan that has them both jumping several feet into the air. It takes a second of panic for Beck to identify the noise's source, and his heart sinks.

"Christ, Dyl," he hisses. "Don't do that, huh?"

Dylan shoots Beck a glare, which quickly melts into an expression of horrified disbelief. It's the exact same expression he wore when he first saw Beck. They all give him a few seconds for the events of the past day to catch up with him. Dylan's gaze swivels from Beck to the unfamiliar apartment to Dana hanging behind him.

That's the moment he finally registers his hangover. He sinks back into the couch cushions, squeezing his eyes shut. "Holy hell," he groans, "where am I?"

"You're in Oz, and I'm the freakin' tin man," Dana says, pressing Cassandra's bottle of radioactive Fanta into Dylan's hands. "Drink that. It'll either kill you or keep you from puking all over us."

"Unless he pukes before he can finish," quips Beck.

Dylan slowly pushes himself up, eyes still screwed shut. "I have an iron stomach." He uncaps the bottle, takes a sniff, and downs it with zero hesitation. To Dylan's credit, he doesn't recoil in horror at the taste; a slight gag gives him away, but he manages to stone-face it all the way down to the dregs of the bottle. He's certainly improved since the days of daring each other to drink whatever horrific concoction the other could throw together in the kitchen. Beck smirks as Dylan slams the empty bottle back down on the table.

"Fuck you," he declares, then grimaces. "Jesus, what *was* that stuff?"

"Who knows?" Dana says. "How do you feel?"

"Like I just drank vinegar. I've been worse, I guess."

Beck feels his eyebrows shoot up. Dylan's the type to stone-face any injury, but when it comes to hangovers he whines hard. For as long as his brother has been able to drink, he's fished for sympathy when caught on the wrong end of a bottle. He doubts that's changed since he's been gone, if the expression on Dana's face is anything to go by. Dylan ought to have a roaring hangover, but he looks bright-eyed and is growing more alert by the minute.

Leaning over to Dana, he finds his friend looking just as baffled as he feels. "You wanna tell me that stuff didn't just work?"

Dana's eyes flutter shut for one moment as she draws in a heavy breath. "Beck, I'll be damned if I have a clue what's goin' on here."

When the door opens again, they're no less taken by surprise. Hastily regaining his cool, Beck straightens himself out from where he'd leapt into Dana's lap (he's not jumpy, the *last* thing he needs is Adam thinking he's jumpy) and stares at the two figures who emerge from the darkened room.

Adam's eyes are shadowed with exhaustion; his face is pinched, brow knit and tense. Cassandra's worn down as well, if her heavy steps and tousled hair say anything, but she also looks pleased with herself. She greets the group with a smile, and Beck feels a knot of tension ease out of his chest.

"Everything went well," she says. "Your friend is just fine."

Dana straightens her shoulders, rising to her feet. "And what's that mean?" she demands. "Is he still two seconds from tryin' to snap our necks like twigs, or is he himself again?"

Beck looks over at Dana, eyes flashing in warning. When Adam clears his throat, even Dylan (who has no idea *what's* going on) snaps to attention.

"Your friend was possessed by a demon, but with my help Cassandra performed an exorcism and cast it out. It's gone now, so your friend's back to himself and is in good shape. His body is exhausted, and his brain's spent. He's gonna have to rest and take it easy for a while. It's gonna feel a little bit like he got run over by a truck for a bit, so I can give him something to help him sleep, but he's gonna be fine. Don't believe me, you can see him for yourselves. He's awake right now, and askin' for you."

For a few moments, no one moves. Beck could almost laugh out loud from relief; his chest feels like it's been filled with balloons, trying to lift him right off the couch. Dana is locked in her own thoughts, gaze boring into Adam's placid expression. At the end of the couch, Dylan has his dark brows furrowed, trying to piece together what little he knows with what he remembers from last night.

He is unable to wait a second longer. Beck jumps to his feet, followed promptly by Dana, and then Dylan. Adam nods at him as they pass each other, and Beck has to resist the urge to hug him. Too much, he knows, and way too soon. He's been pushy enough.

Adam's room is dark, but the figure in the bed is clearly awake. James has himself propped up on the pillows, head lolling against his shoulder, shadowed eyes staring at the doorway. His chest is rising and falling in a steady rhythm. When he catches sight of his friends, he tries to sit up, but Beck moves forward before he can exhaust himself.

"Hey Jimmy, how you feeling?"

If he feels anything like he looks, the answer is a resounding *awful.* Beck won't lie—his friend looks more than worse for wear. James's olive skin is pallid, glistening with sweat. There is a welt on the side of his jaw from where Beck decked him, and scrapes on his bare chest courtesy of his friends dragging him out of the pool. Most striking, however, is the heavy bruising around his eyes. Instead of the shadows Beck had taken them for, he finds that his friend sports two black eyes, swollen and painful looking. However sore the skin looks, James's actual eyes are as clear as ever—warm russet brown, with solid pupils. Utterly human, and utterly *James*.

His friend huffs a breath and tries to smile. "Mmm—like I died 'n came back," he mutters. His words are slurred. Beck notices Dana's lips press into a terse line. "Wanna tell me...what the hell happened?"

Dana steps towards the bed. As soon as her gaze lands on James, a hard tension in her face smooths over. She exhales; all at once, it seems like a great weight has been lifted off her shoulders. The knowledge that her boyfriend tried to kill her was bad enough—but that he wasn't in control of his body or mind at the time, and might not be okay, must have been killing her. Now that her Jimmy is back, she looks as if she's just crossed the finish line of a marathon.

Her manicured hand reaches out to run over her boyfriend's forehead, brushing away the sweat and tension there. "It's okay, honey," she says in a low, sweet voice. "You're fine now."

Instead of being reassured, James just furrows his brow. "Nothing good ever happens when you sound that nice." The (reasonable) wariness draws a chuckle from both Dana and himself; this must hurt something, because he screws his eyes up and sinks back into the pillows. "Uhh... I feel...like I got hit by a bus." he mutters. "Whas' goin' on?"

Contrary to the relief he felt earlier, the anxious ball in Beck's stomach has returned and is growing into something he can't digest. Sure, he might be wisecracking and bantering, but he's still not *himself*—not the same sharp-minded friend Beck is used to. He hasn't seen James this out of it since the time he caught the world's worst flu and was knocked out of commission for a week. His friend looks small and vulnerable in that bed. It's utterly unsuited to James, and Beck can't suffocate the fear gnawing at him.

A sudden touch on his shoulder jars him from his anxiety. He turns, knowing before he even looks that it will be Adam standing there. He looks unruffled, gaze boring intensely into Beck's own. Somehow, that reassures Beck even more than the humanity in James's eyes. "He'll be fine," Adam says in a low voice. "I've got tea ready, to help him get to sleep."

"While he's out, I can cleanse his energy," adds Cassandra from the doorway. "It's no good to have all of that demonic ickiness clinging to him. He'll feel a lot better after that."

Beck inhales a breath, forcing himself to relax. If Adam can be this calm, so can he. "Sure... Just, uh, hang on a minute with that tea, huh?"

"Still have to let it cool," Adam replies. He takes a step back, releasing Beck's shoulder. "Take your time."

In bed, James is still conscious, but his confusion hasn't gone away. His gaze swivels around his bedside, taking in the worried faces of his friends. This can't help calm him down. "Beck? D-Dani? Come on, what's...what's..."

As his gaze settles back on Dana, something in James's face changes. His eyes widen, and his pallid skin seems to go even whiter. His throat bobs as he swallows hard, before a hand lifts in the direction of Dana. "Hey. Baby doll. Did I— did I do something? Dani, are you—I don't *remember* what—"

"Shhh. It's okay, baby," Dana hastens to reassure him, leaning over the bed. "You didn't mean it. It's all right."

The thought of having hurt his girlfriend only upsets James even more. His breathing is starting to grow ragged, and a sense of helplessness is locked around Beck like a vice. He doesn't know how to reassure James after what he's been through. He's not sure any of them do. "I—I don't know... I'm sorry. I didn't—"

No one expects Dylan to push his way to the forefront. Having held himself back until now, the fact that Dylan was even there almost slipped Beck's mind. Dylan didn't see James's attack; he never got a glimpse of his black eyes, and he was barely awake for the midnight ride to Adam's place. He doesn't really know what's going on, but there is no uncertainty on his face as he kneels by James's bedside.

Dylan clasps his friend's hand, twining his fingers through James's own and squeezing. "Don't worry, man. All of us are right here."

James forces himself to focus on Dylan's calm eyes. "O-okay," he says, nodding his head.

"We're not going anywhere, and everything's okay now. Don't freak out on us, okay? You know we've got your back."

James huffs what is almost a laugh, and his lips twitch. "Yeah..." he breathes. "You guys better..."

Footsteps behind them tell the group that Adam has returned to the room, and Dylan waves him over with his free arm. "Here, Adam's just gonna give you something to help you relax," he says, keeping his voice low and reassuring. "It's gonna make you feel better."

"Sure..." The last of the fear ebbs from James's face, and he accepts Dylan's help to push himself upright as Adam holds out the tea. The cup is in his hands within seconds, and the room holds its breath as he takes a sip.

Almost immediately, his shoulders relax. Dylan has to help guide the next mouthful to his lips. By the time the cup is empty, James's eyelids are drooping, and he is ready to melt back into the pillows once more.

Dylan waits until his friend's grip grows slack before pulling his hand away. When he turns to the rest of the group, who have fallen back to the sidelines, he looks solemn but relieved.

Adam and Dana wear unreadable expressions, but Beck is sure his own shock shines clearly on his face. This Dylan is completely different from the boy he remembers. *That* Dylan is still a kid, with the empathy to match. He's never witnessed anything like that from his little brother. Never before has he seen Dylan so soothing, so serious. Ten minutes ago he would have called it impossible.

Maybe it was, for the Dylan who Beck left behind sevem months ago. Not the one he's come back to.

"Nice job, Dyl," he says, for lack of anything better to say. Dylan just ducks his head, accepting Dana's hug of gratitude without a word. He doesn't acknowledge Beck's praise, but Beck didn't expect anything else.

Beck's friends just keep surprising him. How many other ways has everything changed since he's been gone?

"POSSESSION CASES HAVE been cropping up all over since last week. We think it has something to do with the failed necromantic spell, but we aren't sure." Cassandra leans forward, elbows on her knees, and regards the group.

Her tone reminds Beck of a teenage girl sharing a secret, but her expression is more reminiscent of a concerned parent. "If that's the case, it could mean the people coming back to life and the demons running around are related, which would be a bad thing for a whole number of reasons."

Something in Beck's stomach drops out as more than one set of eyes turns to him. He opens his mouth, but Cassandra hears his words before they can leave his lips. "Don't worry, Beck. You're not a demon at all, and you're not possessed. If you were, we'd know. More importantly, *you'd* know."

"Possession is when a demon takes control of your body," Adam cuts in. "You got no free will, no sense of yourself. The *you* who is you is gone, and the demon's in its place. Usually, these cases are rare. We don't know what causes possessions, but the good thing used to be that most demons weren't on earth to try it."

"But now there are more demons around," says Dana, "like the one that just hijacked our friend. Why's that?"

"That's why we think the spell did something bad," Adam says, sighing. "Suddenly demonic activity 'round here is through the roof—and, if we're right, it could be because the barrier between the human and demon world's damaged. Not only would that let demons through to us, it could send all of Hell into war."

Wars? Barriers? Spells? Beck's head is spinning, and his friends aren't faring much better. Dana looks nauseated, and Dylan holds his head in his hands. "This is crazy," he keeps muttering to himself. "This is all *crazy*."

"The thing is," continues Cassandra, "we don't know what's going on in Hell. From what I can sense, which isn't much, feels like there's a lot of unrest down there, but we can't know what's happening for sure."

"All we know is what's going on up here," Adam adds. "And all of a sudden this town's become a hotbed for demonic activity. Seems like there's a demon everywhere you look. They're running around possessing people everywhere, and it's driving folks to do awful things. The world is getting dangerous, and whatever's happening up here is all tied to what's going on down there."

"Which we don't know," chimes in Cassandra. "So essentially—"

"We're fumbling 'round in the dark," Adam finishes, heaving a sigh. "Just trying not to end up dead."

What really interests Beck is Adam—and how he plays a role in this drama. The man seems to know something about everything, and one glance at the papers littering his coffee table tells Beck that he's no ignorant human. There are meticulous notes on everything here, from witchcraft to demons. If Adam isn't a witch himself, then he must be someone like Cassandra.

He can't resist asking. "Where do you play into all this, Adam? What's your job?"

Adams shoulders go stiff. He pauses for a beat too long before replying, voice steely. "I run a bookstore; that's my job. I'm not a witch, and I'm not a psychic. I just know too much for my own good."

The expression on Cassandra's face makes it clear she's heard this explanation before and doesn't quite agree. "Adam is an asset to this town. He's our most knowledgeable source on everything magical," she interjects, an undercurrent of pride in her voice. "He knows all there is to know about magic. More than most witches. More than I do. He's a valuable asset."

Adam ducks his head, uncomfortable with the praise. Beck can't help the way his eyes linger on him. He already respected Adam, but this new revelation casts Adam in a new light—the papers everywhere, the wealth of knowledge of so many things, and the calm in the face of chaos. It makes a lot more sense now, and Beck finds himself in awe of him.

Adam's eyes suddenly flicker up, catching Beck's gaze. Instead of looking away, Beck stares back head-on. Adam holds his eyes, unflinching, and one of his eyebrows quirks in a silent question. Beck feels heat rush to his cheeks.

Cassandra is still talking, but Beck can't hear her. All of his focus is on the dark pools of Adam's eyes. Are they brown? Black? Some impossible shade of midnight that he cannot put words to? He doesn't know, but Adam has a stare that could stop armies in their tracks. Beck finds himself hypnotized, frozen in their sway.

The sudden desire to reach out and touch Adam seizes him. To caress his jaw, to trace the bridge of his nose, to press into the hollow of his throat—just to feel him. It's crazy, but he *wants* to—

The television flickers on with a burst of static, startling Beck into giving a small shout. It only blares for a few seconds before flickering off again. When it does, he finds the rest of the room smirking at him.

"Jumpy, kid," Dana quips. "You're sure gonna scare demons with that yowl of yours. They'll think they're fightin' a little girl."

"Tell your ghost to keep his paws off my TV," Adam says to Cassandra, sounding tired. Cassandra nods, a small smile on her lips. Beck could almost smack himself for forgetting there was a ghost in the room. (Did the ghost notice him staring at Adam?)

"Aren't ghosts supposed to haunt places?" Dylan asks, uncertain.

"They do, generally. Ghosts can haunt what or whoever they like, but usually choose places to get attached to. Don't tell George that, though," Cassandra says, and laughs softly. Not two seconds later, an empty glass slides off of the coffee table and onto the carpeted floor at Cassandra's feet. The beleaguered hauntee rolls her eyes. "Watch it, show-off. You use up all your energy and you're not getting any more from me." Looking up at the group again, she offers them a half-sheepish smile. "He likes being around people."

"A real social butterfly, huh," Dylan murmurs, and freezes in place as if waiting for something to fly at his head. A few seconds pass, filled with nothing; his eyes dart around the room, sharp with anticipation. His expression is funnier than if something had flown at him, and Beck snorts into his palm as Dana reaches over and smacks him.

"Don't antagonize the ghost. You just met him; he doesn't need to know what a dumbass you are already."

Dylan rolls his eyes and looks ready to shoot back something sharp, but Beck clears his throat loudly. "So," he says, raising his eyebrows at Cassandra. "I guess not everyone gets to make friends with ghosts?"

Cassandra gives that same close-lipped smile and taps her temple with one finger. "Psychic," she replies. "I can see, hear, and feel spirits. It extends to demons too, but I've been lucky enough not to have to deal with them."

A psychic—meaning she has to be in tune with the living and the dead. Beck can't help the way he perks up. "Can you see, like...living people's spirits? I mean, if they've...got them."

"I can see energy. Auras, for example." Cassandra fixes him with a stare that quickly turns knowing. "Are you asking for yourself?"

Beck hesitates for a moment, feeling sheepish at being found out. Not that he'd been being very subtle; but Cassandra saw through him so easily that he feels as obvious as a kid looking for a new toy. He can feel a blush creep up to his face as he nods. "Just...do I look normal, ya know? Do I look the same as everybody else?"

Cassandra leans forward and settles her eyes on him. By all rights, Beck knows he should feel uncomfortable. Cassandra's gaze, however, is nonintrusive. Instead of peering into Beck's soul, it's more as if she's reading a book, skimming a cursory glance through the pages and picking out what's notable. The psychic's thoughtful expression doesn't change at all. When she breaks her concentration a moment later, she has a smile ready for Beck.

"You've got a solid aura—bright blue. Your energy is very strong, and very *alive*. Beck, I'd say you're as alive as the person sitting next to you. There's nothing wrong with your energy in any way."

He can't help the grin that breaks out over his face. A weight he hadn't known he was carrying has suddenly vanished, leaving his chest feeling lighter. "That's a relief."

It's stupid, probably—to worry that he's not really alive, even though he can feel his heart in his chest. He wouldn't call himself dead, but the realization that he has died rears its head just when he is almost able to forget it. He still doesn't know how he died, or how he came back—Beck thinks he's justified in being self-conscious.

When Dana clears her throat, all eyes turn towards her.

"So there are demons runnin' around, possessing people—just like Jimmy." She waits for Adam to nod before she goes on. "And this is happening to people all over the city. Why are we not hearing about it?"

"You know all the stuff in the news lately? About people killing themselves, killing others, destroying things?" Cassandra waits for the realization to set in. "That's basically it."

Dana exhales and drags a hand through her mess of curls. "Jesus."

Beck bites the inside of his cheek hard enough that he tastes blood, but that still doesn't stop him from speaking. "So who's doing anything about it?"

"There are professional exorcists," Adam says after a second of reluctance. "Psychics can exorcise too. So can witches. Anyone who knows how can do it."

"Anyone...like us?" Dana suddenly looks very attentive. She is sitting up straight, shoulders stiff and back straight as a rod. There is a spark in her eyes, the same one she gets whenever she talks about project management or corporate domination. It makes her look a little frightening, like she could easily kill someone with a well-placed glare and an overdose of ambition.

Now Adam looks really reluctant. He casts a wary glance at Cassandra before giving a halting nod. "Yeah," he agrees, frowning. "You could, but that doesn't mean you should—"

"I want to learn," Dana says promptly.

Beck gapes at his friend, startled but not really surprised. He expected something like this—Dana is just crazy enough to have seen whatever the hell was in her boyfriend and want more of it. She's probably mad she didn't get a real hit on it. After what the demon did, Dana would be out for her own revenge.

Then, unexpectedly, Dylan pipes up with a low "Me too." Beck's head whips around so fast that he feels something pop.

His jaw drops at the determined look on his brother's face. Dylan is resolute in not meeting anyone else's eyes. His gaze is trained on Adam, and his jaw is set in a way that makes him look older than he is. It's a startling expression to see on his usually mischievous face.

Jesus, thinks Beck. *My kid brother went and grew up without me being around to see it.*

He can feel Dana's elbow digging into his ribs, and Dylan's eyes boring into the side of his skull. He knows when people are waiting for him, and damn him if he's going to let himself get left behind again. "Well, don't count me out," he finally sighs, leaning forward with his elbows on his knees. He offers the two people across from him a smirk. "So, which one of you's gonna teach us how to fight demons?"

Adam heaves a bone-rattling sigh, a look of exhaustion overcoming his face. "You people are gonna be more trouble than you're worth," he mutters.

If Adam is just realizing that now, Beck thinks, he's got a *lot* of catching up to do.

Chapter Four

THE UNFORTUNATE THING about pulling an all-nighter with a bunch of college students on a Sunday night is that college students will inevitably have things to do the next day.

Well, Beck doesn't. He's actually no longer a college student anymore, thanks to the technicality of being legally dead. He's going to have to sort that out real soon, because he has one year left before he gets his degree and he did *not* suffer through political science lectures all these years for nothing.

The school issue doesn't occur to him until around ten o'clock that morning, well after Cassandra's gone home (taking her ghost friend with her), and the entire group has passed out on Adam's couch to get some well-needed rest. Beck is woken up by the sound of Dana's phone alarm blaring, and groggily rolls off of the couch in his flailing to turn off what he can't see.

By the time he's sat up, Dana is already stumbling into her shoes, fighting to drag her fingers through her mess of curls. "Operations lecture," she huffs, wobbling as she comes close to losing her balance. "I've got just enough time to run back home and change—Dylan, *get up*! You've got class too, move it!"

Dylan mutters something incoherent, curled up like a hedgehog on the floor with his ass in the air. This makes it an easy target for the kick Dana aims at him. Dylan lets out a yelp as her foot knocks him flat.

Beck watches on, in a state of groggy bemusement, as his friends rouse themselves and bustle off to their respective classes. James has three classes and a paper due today, but Dana promises to collect what he needs to give her boyfriend time to recover.

With no one else able to stick around, and James still in no shape to go anywhere, it naturally falls to Beck to keep an eye on him. He accepts this task with the solemnity expected of someone still half asleep, waits for the rest of his group to leave, and wastes no time passing out on Adam's couch once more.

The next time he wakes up, it's to the heady scent of bacon frying on a stove.

"Did I wake you?" Adam asks, sounding apologetic. "Sorry. I tried to keep it down as much as possible."

"Let me have some of that food and you can keep me from ever sleeping again." The bacon glistens in the pan, and the eggs beside it look light and fluffy as clouds. Adam's got a plate of freshly cut fruit set on the kitchen counter, and he even poured orange juice into tiny crystal cups. Cutlery is laid out on the table; there are a few books stacked to the side (as is Adam's routine, Beck is starting to realize), but Adam went through the trouble of clearing up.

Beck grins around the rim of his glass as he watches Adam serve the breakfast onto two plates. He's still wearing his reading glasses, and his brow is furrowed in intense focus—like he's tackling long division instead of using a stove. It shouldn't be as funny as it is; it also shouldn't be as attractive. Hey, Beck isn't picky.

"Two mornings now I've woken up here to breakfast," Beck proclaims as Adam slides the plate in front of him. "Be careful. I might never want to leave."

"Not sure how well two people would fit up here. It's a small apartment."

"Don't worry. I'd never think of subjecting your nice place to me for too long. I'm a walking hurricane."

Adam's lips twitch. "Somehow, I'm not surprised."

"What's that supposed to mean?" exclaims Beck, letting out a peal of laughter. Adam does a poor job hiding the smile that tugs at his lips. It makes him look younger, more carefree—and yes, handsome. His grin lights up his face like a dawning sun, and if Beck were a weaker man he'd probably be blinded by it.

(Who's he kidding? He's the weakest man in the world. Adam is giving him tunnel vision.)

"No offense intended," Adam hastens to add. Beck rests his chin in his palm. He takes a slice of strawberry and pops it into his mouth, pursing his lips around the fruit.

"With all the trouble I've been for you, I'm glad you can still joke around." Adam's taking the whole "not-dead guy in his apartment" thing in stride. To be fair, so is Beck, but he doesn't know how else to deal with it. Adam has every right to declare the situation not his problem, but he's been more than willing to help out Beck in every way he's asked. Adam has gone above and beyond. That sort of generosity is unprecedented. "Be honest, are you always this nice to people who barge into your house in the middle of the night?"

"I get those sorts of visitors all the time, obviously." Adam purses his lips. For a moment, he looks so serious that Beck can't help but laugh again. That makes Adam's eyes spark. "But I'm only nice to the ones that interest me."

Beck raises an eyebrow. "I interest you?"

"Very much," replies Adam, unfazed. "You're an interesting person, Beck Murray."

Beck wants to be cool in the face of such praise, but he can feel his face heating up like a firetruck. The curse of blushing easily would be bad enough if he didn't have tissue-paper pale skin, and hair you should only see in cautionary ads about the effects of ginger hair dye. He must really look ridiculous, because Adam takes a sip of juice and almost chokes on it when he can't hold back his laughter.

They go back and forth for about twenty minutes, just talking—and Beck is thrilled to find that Adam is a fantastically easy person to talk to. He goes on about his shop, how long he's had it and what inspired him to start it in the first place. Adam is twenty-five, two years out of college, with a dual degree in English and history. He could have been a teacher but channeled his love for reading into a store instead. The antiques downstairs are mostly local, but the books have come from all over the world. Adam presents a worn old tome that he explains came all the way from India. His shop is his pride and joy.

In exchange, Beck talks about his own life. Compared to Adam's, it seems dull. He's a college student; he lives with his friends; he's got a mom, a dad, and one younger brother; and he's still in the process of figuring out what he wants to do with his life. His favorite sport is lacrosse. Cows scare him. He can't stand swiss cheese.

When he starts talking, he can't seem to stop. He's not even a big fan of talking about himself, but Adam makes it so easy. He hangs off of Beck's every word as if he wants to hear it, and Beck is inspired to go on. He knows he should be talking about more important things...but getting to know Adam, and having Adam know him in turn, seems like one of the most important things of all.

(They avoid the *big* topics. Demons and magic and dead people don't seem appropriate conversation over a homemade breakfast.)

By the time he starts talking about how long he's known James and Dana, a creeping realization has begun to settle upon him. It's a few minutes before it hits him all at once. James.

"Aww, hell," he says; and then, springing to his feet, "Aww, hell! I forgot Jimmy!"

Adam seems to realize the conversation has ended as easily as it began. He's on his feet in the next second, starting to clear up plates from their extended breakfast. "He's right where you left him and doing fine. Last I checked, he was snoring like a truck engine. I don't know when he'll wake up, but as soon as he does, you're free to go."

"Thanks," Beck murmurs, cursing himself for forgetting. His gaze is fixed on Adam's room. "I'm gonna check on him."

"Sure," Adam replies. "I've got work to do downstairs. You know where to find me."

The room is silent as he approaches it, and Beck can feel his heart thrum with anxiety. James is never silent. He is seized with the irrational, awful fear that his friend has vanished—got up and walked away, was possessed again, or worse—but when he pokes his head into Adam's room, he finds James still asleep. Adam had mentioned he would be out for a while to give his body time to recover, so Beck isn't too worried. He checks on him for just a moment. James's face is placid and untroubled. Bruising is still heavy around his eyes, but his breathing is even and he's regained some color back in his cheeks. Appeased, Beck shuts the bedroom door behind him and sets off to track down their host.

He finds Adam right where he expects to—downstairs in the bookshop, working behind the counter. He's got the same reading glasses perched on his nose and casts a dark silhouette in a blue shirt and black slacks. Adam's "business casual" suits him painfully well.

"Everything all right?" Adam calls without looking over his shoulder. His attention is focused on the cash register, where he is thumbing through stacks of bills with an appraising eye. Even when Beck comes up behind him and hoists himself up on the cleared-off countertop, Adam doesn't bat an eye.

"He's still out cold. Guess you're stuck with me today."

Adam casts him a wry glance from the corner of his gaze. "I could think of worse things."

Maybe Beck's in danger of dying all over again, because something about hearing Adam say those words makes his chest feel like it's going to explode. It only lasts for a second before he can breathe again, but he finds a grin on his face as he swings his legs over to the other side of the counter and hops off. The shop is empty, but in the light of day it is well-lit; walls lined with hundreds of books paint the shop in a myriad of colors. Beck can't help but marvel at how nice Adam's shop is. There is a quaintness to it that marks it as a home-run shop, such as the books stacked in the windows and piles sitting on the floor, but it is well-organized, neat, and homey. It reminds Beck a bit of the libraries his mother used to drag him to as a child, only he feels like he could sit in Adam's shop all day (especially if Adam were there to keep him company). He can't hide his curiosity as he turns to inspect the nearest shelf of books.

"Got some pretty cool titles here," Beck remarks. He recognizes none of them. He's not sure he could read any of them if he tried. In response, Adam only offers an amused hum; he's extolled the virtues of his books enough that he probably thinks Beck is sick of hearing him talk about them. Beck could never be sick of Adam.

He spends the next hour meandering around the shop, entertaining himself with whatever catches his attention. All the books on display are normal volumes—biographies, romance novels, serials, and chapter books. There are no books about necromancy or witchcraft to be found. It is, by all appearances, a regular bookstore. Even so, Adam has something to say about everything Beck picks up.

He's settled down to read once or twice, but nothing has lasted. He keeps getting bored with whatever book he picks up, and then turns back to find another. It's happened for the third time. Beck settles the book back where he found it before wandering towards another shelf. Just as he's getting lost in a sea of titles, the chime of a bell suddenly rings throughout the shop.

His first thought is that someone has just walked in. When his gaze swivels to the entrance, two things jump out at him at once: no one has entered the shop, and there is no bell above the door.

Adam has snapped to attention as well. For all of two seconds he gapes at the door with the sort of intensity usually reserved for a dog who's just heard the word "vet." Then he springs into action, so fast that Beck finds himself cringing back even before Adam sprints around the counter and rushes towards him.

"Move, now" is all Adam says, catching Beck by the shoulders and pulling him away from the entrance. Stunned, Beck puts up no resistance as Adam steers him behind the counter and into the hallway.

They bypass the bathroom and closet without a second glance, making a beeline for the final door. Beck has never been inside this room; he's never seen the door open, or even notices Adam acknowledge it in the times they've passed it. Now, without a second of hesitation, Adam throws open the door to a dark room and shoves Beck inside.

"Stay here," he orders. "Don't make a sound, and don't touch anything. Don't go anywhere. Don't breathe too loud."

"So I should just go back to being dead? Or would a corpse in your shop be too obvious?"

"Statues are nice," Adam replies, and at least he isn't in too much of a rush to appreciate Beck's wit. "Be one of those. Just stay here, and stay quiet."

The door shuts behind him, leaving Beck in darkness.

Well, this wasn't the way he wanted to spend his afternoon.

Gritting his teeth, he stares into the pitch black around him and fights to make out anything that could give him a clue as to where he is. The air is stale in here, and the darkness is so heavy that he can't make out a single shadow.

The only plus side to suddenly finding himself blind is that his other senses kick into overdrive, and his own silence enables him to make out sounds coming from the front of the shop. He hears Adam return to the counter, door slamming behind him. Just a few seconds later, the front door creaks with the sound of strangers entering the shop.

"Mr. Clarence, Mr. Bragg," comes Adam's voice, imperturbable as ever. "Nice to see you boys."

"Likewise, Lehexe." The newcomer's voice is rough, a little sharp, like the serrated edge of a knife. "I wish it were on more pleasant business."

"Is there a problem?"

"You could say that." The stranger allows his words to lapse for a moment, and Beck imagines him stepping up to the counter. Is he trying to intimidate Adam, or does he realize he's being cryptic? "I'm sure it hasn't gone over your head—the recent spike in demonic activity. The bar explosion, the earthquake, the uptick in possessions. You've noticed."

"I have." Adam sounds admirably cool. "Not sure what I've got to do with it, though."

"Seems like you know everything, Lehexe," pipes up another voice—a deep, country-roughened baritone. "We were hoping you could help us."

"Anything I can do for the Tresser Corporation, I'll do."

"Of course you will. You're not on their payroll for no reason," says the first voice, a hint of snideness to their tone. Beck can't help the way he flinches—something about the way he says those words pricks like a needle. Why would Adam be on anyone's payroll—and what is the Tresser Corporation?

"Have you heard of anyone coming back from the dead recently?"

The question is so sudden it takes Beck aback. He wishes he could see Adam's reaction—though he doubts the other man's face would change at all. "Can't say I have," Adam replies, and if he's shaken his voice doesn't show it.

"Tresser Corporation is dealing with this problem. We've got reason to believe it's related to the demon surge that's going on. What information can you give us on necromancy?"

"I have some books—" Adam's words cut off with the sound of him fumbling for something. "Here, here...and a few articles, here. That's about all I've got."

"This is it?" The stranger sounds unimpressed.

"I'm a librarian, Clarence, not a miracle worker. Make sure you bring those back when you're finished with 'em." Adam pauses for a beat before asking, nothing but casual, "You fellas tracked down anybody who ain't quite dead anymore?"

"We have." Clarence's answer is clipped. "Like I said, the Tresser Corporation's dealing with them. That's all we're at liberty to say."

"Understood. You boys have a nice day."

Beck almost thinks that's the end of it and is ready to let out a sigh of relief, when Bragg suddenly speaks again. "Lehexe—you hear anything, you call us, all right? Would be a real shame for you to get mixed up in any of this. Those dead folks ain't worth half the trouble they're making."

Beck feels his heart stall in his chest. "They're dangerous?" Adam inquires, tone still neutral.

"We think so. If you see anything, give us a call. You've got our number."

"I'll do that. Tell Mister Tresser I said 'hi.'"

Beck hears the front door open again "Have a nice day, Mr. Lehexe," calls Clarence, and the silence that follows echoes through the store.

Beck stands alone in the dark room, feeling lost and unbearably isolated. Those men had been looking for him. They're searching for the not-dead and came to Adam for information on people exactly like him. He can feel panic leaking like ice water into his lungs. Do they know Adam is hiding something? Could they know he's here? If they find him, what will they do to him? What does Adam have to do with some mysterious corporation, and what—

The light flicks on without warning. The speeding train of questions racing through Beck's mind grinds to a screeching halt, and he spins around, wide-eyed, to find Adam standing in the doorway.

"Easy there," Adam says, unperturbed as ever. "Look like you seen a ghost."

Beck forces the lump of fear back down his throat, unwilling to let it spill out of his mouth. He doesn't want to accuse Adam of anything, and he reminds himself that he has no reason to be afraid of him. Adam just protected him. "What was that about?" he asks instead. Adam shifts on his feet.

"Sorry about that. I didn't want them to know you were here. This seems like the sorta thing Tresser Corps would wanna stick their nose in, and we don't need that kind of trouble."

"What's Tresser Corps?"

Adam doesn't bat an eye. "They make plastic. Come on now, outta there."

It's only Adam's obvious eagerness to get him out of the room that piques Beck's curiosity. He glances around and finds himself startled—he's been shoved into a regular witch's *paradise.*

There's a skull on the nearest table. It looks like an animal skull, but it's still a *skull.* Beck's never seen a real skull up close before, but he's just starting to gape at that when the plants hanging from the ceiling catch his eye. There's a whole rack of greenery dangling towards the ground, different sorts of dried herbs and flowers. Another shelf stacked with herbs stands behind them; mason jars filled with glimmering waters and multicolored crystals litter every other open space in sight. The walls are lined with bookcases, all packed, and multicolored candles are scattered throughout the room.

His mouth drops open, and he gapes around the room without shame. There's so much stuff in here he's never even seen before. He feels like a kid in a toy store. He wants to look at *everything* and doesn't know where to start.

No sooner has he taken one step towards the animal skull, however, than a hand seizes the back of his shirt and starts dragging him. He tries to fight, but Adam has an unexpectedly strong grip. Beck is hauled out into the hallway, door slamming shut behind him.

"Oh man," he breathes, turning to face a glowering Adam. "What was all that stuff? With all that, you've gotta be the best witch around! I thought you said you didn't do magic?"

Beck can *see* Adam bristle, shoulders drawing up like a defensive porcupine. His jaw tightens, eyes flashing with something hot, and Beck only realizes he's made a mistake when Adam spits out the words as if they're burning his tongue. "I don't practice magic. I ain't a witch, and that stuff is none of your business. Stay outta there."

Beck doesn't know how he offended Adam so much, but he's scary when he's mad. "I—I didn't mean—"

"I know exactly what you meant. It's none of your business."

Adam's glare is fierce, and his words are icy. It's a combination that leaves Beck feeling scolded on all fronts, and he wilts like a kicked puppy. "O-okay," he says, taking a step back from an incensed Adam. "I'll just, uhh—go check on James now. Sorry."

He scampers away with his tail between his legs and feels Adam's eyes on him the entire way back up the stairs.

Chapter Five

THINGS ARE AWKWARD with Adam after that.

Beck drives James home later that evening and is relieved to leave the tense atmosphere behind him. Since his temper flared up (perhaps *iced over* would be a more accurate term), Adam has barely spoken to him. Granted, Beck has tried his hardest to stay out of his way too, but the lack of fanfare when he leaves stings. Adam barely even says good-bye; he just watches Beck go, still and silent, from behind the dark rims of his glasses. For the entire ride home, a dull dismay lingers in the pit of Beck's stomach. He feels as if he's messed things up without even realizing.

Had he known Adam would have such a passionate reaction, he never would have asked about the room to begin with—he would have kept his dumb mouth shut. It's too late for that, however. The wedge he's driven between them is as wide as the Grand Canyon, and twice as perilous. Beck doesn't know how to breach it, or if he even should.

He wants to, of course. He's never been the sort of person who can end things on a sour note with someone and take it in stride. He cannot forget Adam, now that he is better than a stranger, and refuses to be shoved to the back of his mind. He would like to make things right, if at all possible.

Knowing *how* is another battle entirely.

When Beck and James return home, Dana is waiting with a pack of beer and a lot of questions. Beck takes advantage of one and ignores the other completely. It is a welcome relief from the burden of his own thoughts. For a long time, he doesn't have to worry about much of anything, except keeping his friends from outdrinking him.

He doesn't realize he left his sweatshirt at Adam's until the next morning; it takes him until noon before he works up the courage to visit him.

Adam is working in his shop, as always, but looks up when Beck steps in. Immediately, his genial customer service face shifts to something more personal, closed off and distant. It couldn't be more obvious that he's not thrilled to see him. Beck's stomach contents curdle, and it has nothing to do with the hangover pounding at the back of his skull.

"I know what you're here for," Adam says, before Beck can even get a word out. "I saw it last night."

"Yeah... I think I left it on your couch? Sorry, I leave a trail wherever I go..." He sounds like an idiot. He knows it, and Adam must be as fed up with his mouth as Beck himself is, because he doesn't even crack a smile as he bends below the counter. When he emerges, he's got a light gray hoodie balanced in one hand.

"Meacon, huh?" he asks as he hands it back. Beck knows he mentioned this to Adam before, but bites his tongue to keep from saying another stupid thing.

"Yup," he says simply. "That's right."

"It's a good school."

"Great."

He takes the sweatshirt from Adam's hands, stumbling back a step as he does so. He's so captured by the way daylight reflects in the dark pools of Adam's eyes that he doesn't notice the vase until he bumps into it.

The crash is awful, but the silence afterwards is worse. Beck gapes down at the shattered porcelain at his feet for a second in mute horror before a rough curse tears from his throat. "Sorry!" he exclaims, dropping to his hands and knees. He scrambles to collect the biggest shards of porcelain in his jacket, allowing smaller pieces to dig into his palms in the process. Another swear escapes him; the floor is littered with dozens of shards.

"I'll clean it up, I didn't mean to, I just wasn't looking—"

He doesn't realize Adam has rounded the counter until he feels him drop down next to him. Adam is so close Beck can feel the warmth radiating from him. It almost knocks him off his feet.

"It's okay," Adam says. He starts to go for the porcelain before noticing the shards in Beck's palms. He winds up ignoring the broken vase entirely, catching Beck's hands to still them.

"It's not a big deal," he insists, forcing Beck to meet his eyes. "It's just fine. Wasn't an expensive vase anyway. It ain't anything to worry about."

Beck swallows and forces himself to exhale. "Right."

Nothing is settled that day. He leaves Adam's shop with his sweatshirt, new cuts on the palms of his hands, and the sense that he's let both himself and Adam down.

Just under a week later, that feeling has not changed. He also hasn't found another excuse to go back to Adam's place, and isn't sure he wants to. Whatever has gone awry between the two of them, Beck feels paralyzed by it. It's not a sensation he likes. (He's dead, for God's sake! What is he so afraid of?)

He tries searching Adam's name on impulse, hoping his online presence might give him a clue to what Adam is all about. There's nothing; no Twitter, no Facebook, not even an ancient Myspace profile. Not that he'd taken Adam for much of a social media guy, but there's no trace of him online whatsoever. *Lehexe's Books* doesn't even have a website. Beck hadn't known it was *possible* for someone to leave absolutely no virtual footprint. Once again, Adam is an enigma.

It feels like he's hit a dead end. The chance to make things right with Adam has come and gone. Beck is left with no way to figure out what the hell is going on with him—and the memory of Adam's dark stare remains seared into his mind.

HIS SECOND CHANCE shows up on his doorstep on a sunny Sunday morning, less than a week after Beck came back to life.

The last thing he's expecting at nine o'clock is for the chime of a doorbell to ring throughout the house. If he's being honest, he's a little annoyed. Most of their friends know that showing up at their house at any time before noon, for any reason, won't go over well. They're busy college students. Dragging them out of bed before they must be awake by necessity is as easy as moving mountains. Anyone who dares disturb them runs the risk of facing fire and brimstone for it. (Beck has witnessed Dana's "running-on-nothing-but-three-hours-of- sleep-and-spite" wrath firsthand. The memory still makes him shudder.)

Beck has no clue why their visitor is apparently ignorant of this fact, but he sure doesn't enjoy dragging his sorry ass out of bed this early in the morning. His hair is a tangled ginger bird's nest, his eyes are still crusty with sleep, he's in his boxers, and he's got morning breath strong enough to kill a cow. When he opens the door, he squints against the bright light.

The last person he expects to find standing on their doorstep is a petite brunette with a wide smile and a canvas bag slung over her shoulder.

"Good morning, Beck!" Sophie chirps. Her smile widens when she sees the realization dawn on Beck's face. "Sorry for just dropping by, but I've got a few things I thought you might like. You haven't had breakfast, yet? I would have dropped by earlier, but I figured that was too early. Mind if I come in?"

The onslaught of words is too much for Beck to deal with when he's barely awake to begin with. He can't think of anything else to do, so he just opens the door wider, allowing Sophie clear entry into the house. "Yeah," he mutters. "Sure."

"Wonderful!" Sophie's grin is brighter than the early morning sun. She brushes past Beck into the house, leaving the scent of cherries behind her. "Oh, I love your house! Who decorated? It's beautiful!"

"I... I have no clue." Beck shuts the door. The force causes him to tilt sideways, and he winds up slumped against the wall. Sophie glides down the hallway into the kitchen, wide eyes taking in her surroundings. All Beck can think is that he *seriously* needs to put pants on.

"I'm gonna," he says. "Um. You know."

Sophie's settled herself at the kitchen table and is already unloading things from her bag—flour and butter, it looks like. She waves him off, still smiling, like nothing about this is weird at all. Dazed, Beck leaves her to it and stumbles back up the stairs.

He brushes his teeth, combs his hair, and gets dressed in record time; he even adds a tiny spritz of cologne for good measure. (Sophie is Adam's friend; he can't have her thinking they all live here like cavemen.) By the time he gets back downstairs, Sophie has James's nonna's mixing bowls spread across the table and is peering over them like a scientist.

"What do you think?" she says, glancing up at him. "Cookies first? It's not your traditional breakfast food, but I've got all the stuff. Then I was thinking muffins. Nice, don't you think? Turning the usual 'meal before dessert' thing on its head. Something different!" Her lyrical accent carries her words like a song. Beck is still too busy trying to figure out what's going on here to form a coherent reply.

"Hang on. You showed up here first thing in the morning...to bake for us?"

"No." Sophie points a long spoon at him like a magic wand. "I showed up to teach you how to bake. You mentioned you wanted to when we met, remember?"

Beck does remember; but he certainly never asked for this. He hasn't seen Sophie since that morning in Adam's house, so how on earth...

"I guess," he mutters, frowning. "I've never learned, though. I'm bad at it."

Sophie's eyes glitter. "You remember what I told you? Anyone can bake." She claps her hands together, bouncing on her heels. Her exuberance is irrepressible. "Now, let's get to it!"

What's Beck supposed to do, argue with her? She's got all the ingredients laid out in front of him. She even brought her own *spoons*, for chrissakes. He could kick her out, but...at this point, what would that prove?

He sighs and steps around the table. "You're the boss," he tells her. "What do we do first?"

As it turns out, Sophie isn't just a good teacher; she's *excellent*. Beck has always been hopeless in the kitchen, but she walks him through each step in a way that makes it impossible for even him to screw up. She doesn't get annoyed when he gets eggshell in the bowl. She only laughs when he accidentally spills oil on the table. When she steals a handful of chocolate chips from the bag when he isn't looking, he calls her out, and she responds by tossing a chip at his head. (He catches it in his mouth, making her shriek in delight.)

By the time they get the cookies on the pan, things have stopped being awkward. They managed to overcome the weirdness of this sudden visit and have fallen into a pleasant rhythm. Sophie is as easy to talk to as before. She's quick, she's funny, and she doesn't take herself too seriously. When Beck asks how she learned where he lives, she reminds him that they share a mutual acquaintance in Dylan. He once mentioned he lives in a big red house on Unity Lane with his roommates; she was able to fill in the blanks.

"How good is your memory?"

"I don't forget things. It's a curse." Sophie shrugs and steals a bite of cookie dough out of the bowl.

By the time they get the cookies in the oven, Beck can hear the rest of the house start to stir. It won't be long before they won't be alone anymore; already he can hear James's heavy footsteps as he plods his way to the shower. He figures they'll have enough time for the cookies to bake before anyone gets down here (especially if James and Dana are in a frisky mood), so it leaves he and Sophie enough time to chat.

"So, you showed up here...because you wanted to teach me how to bake. You just had to. Is that right?"

Sophie catches his eye and smirks at him. "I kept looking in my baking cupboard and thinking of you, I'll admit. You were haunting me."

Beck snorts. "Right." He leans against the table, stealing a scrap of cookie dough from the nearby bowl. His finger makes a wet sound when he pops it into his mouth. "Come on."

Sophie sighs, shrugging in a single, languid motion. "Adam told me about the argument you had. He was upset about it. I thought I'd stop by and...see if there was anything I could do."

Beck falters, his expression shifting from amusement to something darker. Thoughts of Adam have been plaguing him all week long. Still, he never expected anyone else to get involved, especially not Adam's friend. Is there a possibility Adam could have asked Sophie to talk to him?

As if reading his mind, Sophie shakes her head. "He doesn't know I'm here. I'd appreciate you not telling him. He says I'm too nosy."

"A little nosiness can be an okay thing." Beck forces a smile; Sophie grins back, relieved.

"So, what happened?"

He sighs. "I don't know. He shoved me into a room filled with all sorts of witchy stuff, and when I started asking him about it, he went all snappy. Like I stepped into a bear trap or something. I didn't mean to hit a sore spot, but I'm gonna be honest, I don't know what I did."

Sophie regards him for several long seconds, expression unreadable. It isn't long before she starts bustling around the kitchen, clearing away baking scraps and bowls they are no longer using. After a moment, she speaks.

"Adam and witchcraft have...a complicated relationship."

Beck crinkles his nose. "Isn't he supposed to be some kind of expert on it?"

"He is. He knows as much as a person can know." Sophie's pink lips twitch up in a small, fond smile. "But he is a scholar, not a scientist. He will theorize, but never put them to the test. He has his own reasons for not doing magic. When they are challenged, he can get...defensive."

Her tone implies she knows this firsthand, and Beck sees a window. Maybe he can learn a little more from his friend about what Adam is reluctant to share. If anything can help him understand the enigmatic man better, he'll take it. "What *are* his reasons?"

Sophie drops what she's doing and turns to face him. Her expression is placid, unreadable. "I can't tell you everything, Beck. I don't *know* everything. I can't give you all the answers to Adam."

Beck sighs, slumping forward. He feels as if he's being crushed by an Adam-sized weight on his chest; all he wants to do is lighten the load. "Give me something," he says. "Please."

Something in Sophie's expression softens. She folds her fingers together, gazing down at them. "Adam comes from a very prestigious magic family. His mother was a witch. His father was an exorcist...and from what I understand, the profession didn't end well for him."

Beck exhales in a single rush of breath. Sophie nods, recognizing understanding in his eyes. "His reasons are complicated, and I can't claim to understand him. Sometimes it seems as if...as if he's yearning to do magic. As if it's what he's meant to do, and he knows it. Still, he has always turned his back, every single time."

"His willpower's a damn beast," Beck mutters. Sophie lets out a peal of laughter.

"Hey," he says, and she turns to him. She almost looks apprehensive, before he allows a genuine smile to take over his face. He sees the moment her shoulders slump, no longer tense but relaxed once again. "Thank you. I want to make things better."

"I think you should." Sophie nods. "Be his friend, at least. He cares for you already. I believe he'd be willing to let you in."

Beck sure wouldn't slam that door in his face. He exhales, shaking his head, before turning back to the table.

The problem of Adam can be sorted through later. He's still got clean-up to do.

By the time the kitchen looks good as new again, he and Sophie have lapsed into silence. She seems content enough, but Beck has never been comfortable with silences. They make him antsy. His mind starts to wander, and he tends not to like the places it wanders to.

Like now, for example. He can't help but recall a conversation he heard nearly a week prior. Until today, he'd almost pushed it from his mind. Now, with Sophie right next to him, it rushes back full-force.

(Cassandra's head is bowed over her cup of tea. Her brows are furrowed; the corners of her mouth are tight. She looks as tentative to ask the question as Beck is to overhear it, but the words leave her lips all the same. "Adam. How is Sophie? I talked to her the other night, and she felt so—" She pauses, teeth dig into her lower lip. "—stressed."

Adam shrugs and exhales, sprinkling a liberal amount of honey into his teacup. "She's doing as fine as she can be. Of course she's worried."

"About Alyssa?"

"You know anything else that can get under her skin like that?"

Adam holds her gaze for a moment longer, before Cassandra sighs. She shakes her head, ponytail bobbing, before turning away. Adam stirs the honey into the tea, a look of concentration taking over his face. That's when Beck is able to turn away.

Sophie—who was so worried about the girl who followed Adam into the apartment. Alyssa has been skittish as a doe, not daring to speak up during Beck's entire revelation. He got the sense she and Sophie were close, but why would Sophie be worried about her friend?

Something in the way her name was spoken struck him too. Alyssa, as if the word is taboo, forbidden. What could be so wrong with Alyssa that it worried not just her friend, but Adam and Cassandra as well? What could be wrong with Sophie that it leaves her friends looking consumed by unease?

Beck doesn't have a single answer. Even so, the conversation swirls in his head for the rest of the night.)

Sophie is standing in his kitchen, right here and now. It's hardly the best time, Beck knows, but if he doesn't ask, there's a chance he might never get an answer. Sophie *seems* normal enough to him, but then again, he barely knows her. If something's bothering her, maybe he could help.

"So, umm—can I ask a question? It might be nothing, I don't know, I just..."

"You want to ask anyway? Which means it's clearly on your mind, which makes it important enough to voice. Besides, nothing is nothing." Sophie glances at him, a smile tugging at the corners of her lips. "Whatever you want to ask."

Beck bites his lip. Sophie's trust is given so easily; a question like this almost feels like he's breaking it. "Is it," he begins, then hesitates. He needs a different tactic. No use beating around the bush. "I heard Adam talking a few days ago, you know. About you. He sounded really worried. And look, I get it's not my place, but...is everything okay?"

Sophie blinks at him for a second too long before she takes a deep breath. Her face is blank. "Of course it is. Why wouldn't it be?"

"Because...of Alyssa?" Memories of Adam's outburst flash through his mind. Beck flinches, as if expecting a physical blow. To his surprise, however, Sophie just goes still for a long moment before a close-lipped smile spreads across her face.

"Everything is fine with Alyssa," she replies, and huffs what cannot be called a laugh. "Adam worries about everything. She hasn't...been herself lately, but we're dealing with it. Soon enough, she'll be back to normal."

Sophie speaks with conviction, but there's some underlying current in her tone that throws Beck off. She sounds anxious, uncertain—as if her words do not have the effect on herself that she desires for Beck.

Beck opens his mouth, about to say as much; then he thinks better of it. He doesn't want to push. If Sophie says everything is all right, then he believes her. "I'm glad to hear it," he says instead. "I hope she gets better soon. If I can do anything—"

"No," Sophie says, a bit too quickly. She seems to realize it too, because she pauses, bites her lip, then sighs to herself. "*Ça ne sera pas facile*," she mutters; then, just as quickly as she grew still, she pulls herself out of it. The placating smile she summons is clearly for Beck's benefit. "She's doing fine as things are right now. Thank you, though."

She offers him a genuine smile. Beck cannot help smiling back.

"How have you been?" she asks then, so nonchalantly that the non sequitur almost seems natural. "After everything? It's been a week, hasn't it?"

"Just about. Yeah, I feel...fine, I guess. I feel fine. A couple headaches, but I'm pretty good. Nothin' to complain about."

Sophie's eyes narrow. "Have you had any mood swings? Any feelings that you can't explain?"

The atmosphere has suddenly shifted—from lightness to something heavier, tense in a way that Beck can't explain. It's not like Sophie is interrogating him, but there is an undercurrent to her question that makes him feel like there's more to her words than what she says. He feels hesitant to answer.

"Uhh, no? Nothing like that."

"Are you sure?"

"I—"

Just then, the oven dings, and the timing has never been better. The tense atmosphere shatters like a pane of glass. A weight lifts from Beck's chest when the scary focus on Sophie's face vanished as quickly as it appeared. She springs forward, lighting up in delight as she glimpses the assembly of golden cookies in the oven.

"Perfect!"

She instructs Beck to get a plate and busies herself removing each cookie from the pan. They are warm and dripping with chocolatey goodness; just looking at them makes Beck's stomach clench in hunger. He reaches for one as soon as it's on the plate, but Sophie swats him away with a teasing admonishment to "wait your turn!"

Once the pan has been cleared, Beck is finally allowed to go wild. He pounces on the cookies.

"Oh my God," he moans around a mouthful. "Oh. Wow. This is *amazing.*"

Sophie beams. "I'm glad you like them!"

The thing about baking cookies is that the smell is inescapable. It's like fumigating your house with sheer heaven; naturally, it isn't long before the rest of Beck's roommates start to flock downstairs like vultures to a dying cow. Their initial reaction is to be wary of the stranger in their kitchen. Then they spot the plate of cookies, and that's when Sophie becomes another member of the family.

Beck had known he wouldn't be able to keep the cookies to himself for long, but he did not anticipate the sheer voracity with which his friends would attack the product of his (okay, mostly Sophie's) hard work.

James has three cookies in his hand and is shoving them in his mouth one after the other. Looking at him, you'd think he was raised on a barn—even though Beck knows his mother would scream at him if she ever saw her baby boy being such a pig. Dana's got more manners, but she's busy trying to steal cookies from her boyfriend's hands whenever she gets the chance.

"Hey, watch it!"

"How many have you had? Stop hogging 'em all!"

"Steal from me again and your shampoo's gonna end up with glue in it!"

"I'll soak your toothbrush in vinegar, *cariño*, just try me."

Dana snatches another cookie right out from under James's nose. His eyes bulge, and in his rush to scramble for it back, he almost knocks over the kitchen table. Beck watches, unimpressed, cradling his water bottle to keep it from being knocked over. Sophie looks torn between confusion and concern.

"Are they always like this?"

Beck shrugs. "Sometimes they're worse."

The combination of Dana and Jimmy is like a match forged in hell—two confident, stubborn, passionate people who don't know how to take "no" for an answer. In the interest of preventing the Apocalypse, they probably should have been kept hundreds of miles away from each other. Instead, they decided to fall in love. They've been unstoppable ever since.

It wouldn't even be so bad, except Beck has to live with them.

Sophie, whose remarkable talent for making friends continues to go unmatched, quickly drags James and Dana into her orbit. James isn't friendly to strangers to begin with, but even he cannot help grinning at Sophie's wry humor or praising her baking skills. ("You kept Beck from settin' the kitchen on fire—that's a miracle on its own.") Dana takes to her newest acquaintance like a duck to water, and it isn't long before she and Sophie are sitting across from each other, trading stories about school and friends like they've known each other their whole lives.

"That's how I got my scholarship. Full ride, baby." Dana slaps her hand down on the table, grinning; Sophie mirrors the expression. (When she's not being a pain, Dana's pride can almost be endearing.)

"So you chose to come to this school because your boyfriend goes there?"

"Wrong. I chose Meacon because it's got one of the best business management programs in the country. Having this one around was just an added bonus."

"Hey!" James protests. Dana shoots him a grin that belies her spoken callousness. Beck can't help but roll his eyes; this is the stuff he has to live with.

"Do you like cooking?" Sophie asks. Dana scoffs around a mouthful of cookie.

"Gimme a pot of water, I can set it on fire."

"I call that a talent in itself," Sophie replies, and Dana laughs.

By the time Dylan stumbles downstairs, bleary-eyed and bedheaded, it's past eleven o'clock. Sophie straightens up immediately, greeting him with a light "Hi, Dylan."

Dylan stops cold and gapes at Sophie like she's some sort of ghost. The awkward moment stretches on for long enough that even James starts looking uncomfortable, until Sophie finally clears her throat and forces her smile to stay on her face.

"I know it's been a while. I just stopped by to talk to Beck... I made cookies. Would you like some?"

Dylan slowly straightens up and shakes his head. His eyes flicker from Beck to Sophie. Beck sees the moment they darken, realization clouding his face. "No thanks," he replies. "I'm okay."

Sophie opens her mouth to say something else, but she's too late—Dylan is already darting out of the kitchen like he can't move fast enough. Her face falls, and Beck can't help feeling bad for her.

Dana and James exchange glances; finally, Dana says loudly, "So, what's the recipe for these?"

Recipes and phone numbers are exchanged before Sophie is at last ready to leave. Beck helps her bundle everything back into her bag by showing her to the door. She looks worn down, in a way. Out of the bright light of the kitchen, he can't help but notice the knot that tugs at her brows, the way her eyes seem shadowed, as if she hasn't been getting as much sleep as she ought to. A flash of worry hits him, but he forces himself to push it aside. He thanks her for stopping by, "even if it was just to see how awful at baking I am."

Sophie smiles and shakes her head. She is halfway out the door before she stops.

"Beck," she says, "have you figured out how you died yet?"

It is as if the entire morning has been leading up to this one question; the inquiry slices through Beck's armor like a scythe. Sophie's expression is guileless, but she knows. She *must* know; otherwise, she would not be asking. Beck's death and resurrection is a cloud that has been hanging over all of them for days, but the exact nature of how he died is a topic no one has dared to bring up. James and Dana steer clear of the topic; Dylan's lips are welded shut. Even Adam has not brought up the issue, and doesn't seem inclined to.

Beck doesn't know. He has *no idea* how he died.

He says nothing, but his mouth hanging open in surprise is answer enough. Understanding shines from Sophie's face. She lowers her head and reaches out to give his hand a squeeze. Her touch is warm, gentle as a caress.

"Maybe you should find out," she tells him. "Maybe...things will be different if you know."

She leaves him there without another word. Beck is left staring, her final words echoing in his head, as Sophie makes her way down the walkway. Once Sophie is gone, he is left alone.

Chapter Six

THAT NIGHT AT dinner, he cannot taste a thing. His friends' voices are nothing more than droning background noise. A headache pounds at the back of his skull; if he focuses too hard on it, he imagines he can hear whispers in its low hum.

He finds himself holed up in his room before the rest of his friends have cleared out of the kitchen. He's glad to be back, but he can't chatter and be boisterous when there's so much chaos swirling around in his head. There's so much he can't make sense of, and so much he's still struggling to understand. With just a few words, Sophie seems to have broken those floodgates down. Now he can no longer hold any of his questions back.

The Tresser Corporation agents said that he could be "dangerous." Dangerous *how*? Beck hasn't been feeling any violent impulses or compulsions outside of what he'd call his own. Cassandra told him his energy was fine. If no one is influencing him, how could he possibly be dangerous?

Even if he isn't acting out of character, Dylan *is*. His brother has been reticent, reserved, and downright mean since Beck got home. Beck's very presence seems to set him off, and Dylan has made it clear he wants nothing to do with him anymore. Hearing those words stung in a way Beck could never have been prepared for, but seeing Dylan withdraw from everyone and go out of his way to avoid him hurts more. It's like his kid brother has become a completely different person in the time Beck has been gone, and he doesn't understand what's happened.

Finally, his own death. This is the mystery that won't leave him alone. It plagues his thoughts. When he closes his eyes, he imagines different ways it could have happened; when they are open, he looks around and wonders what the world was like when he wasn't here. His friends seem normal now that he's back, but he gets the feeling this is a front. Things are not the same as they were; they cannot be. No one seems willing to bring up Beck's actual death. Any time he's brought up calling his parents, someone's warned him against it. It's like they're...trying to keep the truth from him. Then again, Beck hasn't asked. Maybe he was afraid; maybe the same mental block keeping him from asking questions kept that shoved to the back of his mind too, until Sophie.

Now he wants to know. He can't *not* know. If his death is the key to all these mysteries, then he *can't* ignore it any longer.

At a loss, he turns to his generation's failsafe: the internet. He soon finds himself lost in the depths of Google, trawling through results for any sort of answers. His first attempt is to Google himself. The only results the name *Beck Murray* brings up are his own obituary, plus an old article about his high school graduation that mentioned his name. Discouraged, he then turns to searching up other things, like the bar explosion from a few weeks ago, and the earthquake that shook the town. It all happened, just like he was told— and he wasn't here for any of it.

Only when he searches up necromancy does he really fall down the rabbit hole, and it's not long before he's lost in lengthy articles detailing in-depth procedures to summon the dead.

It's a lot more complicated than it seems. Necromancy is nothing like movies and TV shows led him to believe. It isn't really about bringing the dead back to life. People who practice necromancy talk to the dead, worship them, communicate with them. They form connections with spirits. They learn about the "other side," wherever that may be, and some even travel there. They work with the dead, but from everything Beck reads, it's impossible to bring someone back. Magic doesn't work that way. It isn't that strong.

Which can only mean that people coming back from the dead isn't magic at all, but something *else*.

Beck is so focused on his research he doesn't even realize someone has opened his door. Footsteps are muffled against his plush carpet. He does not realize he's no longer alone until a shadow falls across his screen. It almost scares the life out of him, again.

"You're still up?" James demands. His frown morphs into exasperation as he stares down at Beck's startled face. "And having a nervous breakdown. Go figure."

Beck swings a punch at James's ribs. "Don't do that!"

"What? It's the middle of the night, and your light's still on. What do you want me to do?"

Beck glances up in surprise, then down at the time on his laptop. It's nearly one in the morning. He looks at James again, sheepish, and offers a tiny "oh" that has his friend rolling his eyes.

"I dunno if zombies need sleep, but get some anyway."

"Could say the same thing to you, Emily Rose."

James snorts and pushes his way farther into the room. Beck's bedroom floor is the same warzone it was when he left it seven months ago. He can *feel* the discomfort radiating off of his best friend. James is a neat freak. It's a surprise to everyone who meets him, but a godsend to the disorganized college students who live with him. James's lips twist in a sneer as he catches sight of a pair of discarded boxers half buried under Beck's bed. "You realize you've probably got ten types of mold in here. We should've cleaned the place up."

"Why didn't you?" Not that Beck isn't grateful to find his things all where they should be, but half a year is a hell of a mourning period.

"I wanted to. So did Dana, after a while. It was Dylan who wouldn't let us. Hell, he was going crazy. *'Don't go near Beck's room,'* he kept saying. *'No one touches Beck's stuff.'* So we didn't."

Beck huffs and frowns down at the screen again, filing this information away for later. If Dylan was so dogged about defending his memory, why can't he stand to look at him now?

James takes a seat at the corner of Beck's bed and draws his feet under him as if he expects something on the floor to bite him. Beck would mock him for it, if he were in the right mood. Not now, though. He's tired, he's confused, and he's not sure he wants James to leave him alone or stay right here.

"Come on, Beck," his friend says after it becomes clear Beck isn't about to tear his head out of his laptop. "Shut it down."

Beck nudges him away when James reaches for the computer, but his friend is persistent. He takes the laptop and closes it, placing it with care at the foot of Beck's bed. Beck pouts like a petulant child, but James shoves his shoulder.

"Sleep. Ever heard of it?"

"I can't get to sleep," Beck mutters. "I kinda wish I had some of Adam's sleep tea right about now. At least that might put me out."

"Don't go turning into an addict on us now. We just got you back," James grumbles. He pulls back the blankets of Beck's bed and looks at him pointedly. For a moment, Beck can only gape—is James seriously trying to tuck him in like a baby? When James doesn't flinch, however, Beck mutters under his breath but slips beneath the covers.

Sure enough, James pulls the comforter up to Beck's chin. "There. Snug as a...bug, or something? Is that the expression? I dunno." He looks defiantly pleased with himself. "Now, get some sleep."

James turns away, and Beck can't help the rush of questions that flood back into his head. He knows he shouldn't say anything, but he can't hold himself back. He spits the words out before he can think better of them.

"Jimmy, how did I die?"

James freezes in Beck's doorway. For a long second, no one dares to move. Silence hangs over the room like a shroud, paralyzing them.

When James turns, his expression is closed off. Beck feels the spark of hope in his chest sputter and die. As long as James looks like that, no information will be pulled from him.

"Don't do that," James says. "Don't start with that, Beck."

"Come on, please," he sighs, an edge of desperation leaking into his voice. "I've gotta know."

"If you can't remember, you don't need to," shoots back James, and he looks fierce—defensive again, like Beck is someone who needs to be protected. "Just trust me."

A spark of anger ignites inside of Beck's chest and surges up his throat, hot enough to burn. How can he trust anyone when no one is willing to *tell him* anything? He opens his mouth, ready to give his friend a piece of his mind—

But James shuts the door behind him before he can get a word out.

BECK ISN'T SURPRISED to find himself in the doorway of the bookshop the next day. Glancing up from a book on the counter, Adam doesn't seem to be either.

"Adam," says Beck, "I need to remember how I died."

Adam stares at him for a long, hard moment, before he sighs. His book slams shut. "Well, don't just stand there. Shut the door behind you."

AFTER THE THIRD time Sophie's cell phone goes to voicemail, Adam lets out an agitated grunt and slams his phone down on the counter. Beck can't help but wince at the abuse of technology, but Adam looks testy enough he isn't willing to try his temper by saying anything.

"This isn't like her," Adam mutters, more to himself than Beck. "She treats that phone like a baby. Always has it on her."

"Maybe she's letting it charge," Beck suggests, not seeing why Adam would be so worried. It's not unusual for people not to answer their phones—even Beck has replied to texts a week later more than once. Adam's brow is furrowed, however, and he looks genuinely distressed at his friend's failure to pick up.

This frustration, at least, Beck can empathize with. Though Adam is willing to help him get his memories back and knows a spell that would do it—in fact, it seemed like he'd been expecting the request—Adam has made it very clear he won't be performing the spell himself. For that, a witch would be needed. Adam isn't a witch, he doesn't practice magic, so they would have to give Sophie a call.

(He only declared these facts once, but Beck still winced when he said them. The last thing he wants to do is press Adam's button again. He's learned from last time.)

If Sophie isn't answering, however, their plans fall through. Sophie is Adam's go-to witch, and when Beck suggested he could try calling someone else, the way Adams's face fell suggested that wasn't an option. Adam seems like a private person to begin with; Beck wouldn't be surprised to find that he has a small pool of friends.

"I just hope she's okay," mutters Adam. He's staring down at his phone like he expects it to ring any second, and he looks worried in a way Beck hasn't seen before. He doesn't think before he reaches out and places a hand on Adam's shoulder, giving him a quick but firm squeeze.

"Hey, don't worry. If that won't work, we can find another way."

Adam seems focused on Beck's hand touching him; for a moment, Beck wonders if he's even heard what he said. Then, with deliberate slowness, Adam reaches up, lays a hand over Beck's own, and detaches it from his shoulder.

"I wish I could help you on my own, Beck," he says, meeting Beck's eyes again. "I'm sorry."

It's the answer Beck was expecting, but he can't help the way his heart sinks anyway. Hand burning from the feeling of Adam's touch, he shoves it into his pocket and heaves a sigh. Adam had been his best bet. Without his help, Beck doesn't know how he's going to find out what happened to him. Dylan isn't even talking to him, James has already clammed up, and Dana can keep a secret like her jaw's been wired shut. He'll have no luck at home.

"Isn't there something else? Anything." he says, voice edging on desperate. "We could wait for Sophie. Hell, I'll do the spell myself if you tell me how. Just gimme an instruction guide and I'm set."

Adam's lips twitch, just shy of a smile. Instead, he quirks his eyebrow. "So you know how to direct energy?" Beck's answering stare is blank. "Summon memories? *Meditate*?"

"Uhh...is that some sort of cooking thing?"

That really does make Adam crack a smile. Beck is hit with a flash of victory, brief but poignant. Even if he gets nothing else from this day, he's still made Adam smile. "It's a two-person spell, Beck. You couldn't do it on your own, though I've got no doubt you'd try."

"Then we just gotta find another person. What about Cassandra?"

"She's a psychic, not a witch."

"Psychic's good enough, right?" Beck can see on Adam's face that it is not. "What about Sophie's friend? Allie, or Ashley, whatever her name was—"

"Alyssa can't help us either. She's just like you."

Beck stares at Adam for a long moment. Realization settles upon him, creeping into his body like a winter chill.

"Just like me as in, 'has no clue what the hell is going on' or just like me as in 'not dead'?"

Adam sighs, and it's all the answer Beck needs. "Sophie found her a night before we found you. They were college friends. Alyssa's been dead for just a few months. How do you think we knew what to do with you?"

A tiny, half-hysterical laugh bubbles up Beck's throat. So *that's* why Sophie kept looking after Alyssa like a concerned mother. Knowing there are other people like this is a relief, but...

"Does *she* remember how it happened?"

"I don't know, Beck." Adam holds up his hands, defensive. "I don't know. Alyssa's Sophie's responsibility, and somehow you've become mine."

The words cause indignation to glare up in Beck's chest. He's *no one's* responsibility but his own. "Then why won't you help me?"

"I want to!"

"But you're not! Why? Are you scared, or do you just not care?"

Adam opens his mouth, ready to fire back—then he pauses. He takes a deep breath, jaw clenching and unclenching, before replying in far a calmer tone, "You don't know what you're asking."

Beck knows exactly what he's asking. He's asking for his goddamn life back.

This is the first time he's been so close to answers about his death. He can't walk away now, not when he's just a spell away from figuring out what's going on. The chance to find answers is within arm's reach, and he can't let it slip through his fingers. No one else seems to get it, but there is a desperate *need* to know burning inside Beck's chest, growing fiercer with each second.

If Adam could just *understand*...

Thirsty for empathy, Beck looks to Adam—who has his frown trained down at a book on the counter, studiously avoiding his gaze. Beck feels a burst of desperation.

"Adam, I can't give up on this. I just—*can't*. I don't have a life anymore, and I don't even remember what *happened*. I'm never going to be able to live until I remember how I died. Not knowing—God, it's eating at me, and I can't stand it for much longer. Everyone's acting like I shouldn't know, but I *have* to. So, I'm asking you—please. Help me. Isn't there anyone else we could call to do the spell? Someone else you know, *anyone—*"

Adam cuts him off by turning, abruptly, and opening the door behind him once more. He doesn't look back at Beck as he slips into the hallway. Baffled, Beck trails after him, and his eyes widen once he realizes where Adam is headed.

"Uhh—" Adam pauses, his hand on the doorknob to the room. The Room, the one that Beck was under the assumption he should never look at again. Suddenly he's not sure if he should have followed Adam at all. "What're we doing?"

Adam's dark-clad shoulders heave with a sigh. "Well, Beck," he says, turning to face Beck again. "I'm gonna help you with this. So you can hang out in the hallway, or you can come in here; it's your choice."

Beck can't help the massive grin that spreads across his face, like a flower opening up to the sun. At once the world around him seems that much brighter, and the man in front of him even more amazing. Instinct drives him forward before he can stop himself, and he catches Adam up in a tight embrace.

"Thank you," he exclaims against Adam's shoulder. For several long seconds, Adam is stiff in his arms.

Then Adam's shoulders relax, ever so slightly. Only when Beck catches a glimpse out of the corner of his eye does he realize Adam is smiling too.

"Come on," he says, voice low and warm. "You want that spell or not?"

ONCE THE SPELL gets underway, Adam reveals himself to be scarily competent at this whole magic thing.

Beck thinks he could watch Adam draw chalk circles on hardwood floors for days. It's not just how good he looks hunched over (though he *does*) but Adam's hands work with a smoothness Beck could never hope to emulate. Every movement is sure, every twitch of a finger precise and unfaltering. Adam had beautiful hands, and Beck is so caught up watching him work that he doesn't realize the circle is done until Adam stands up and says to him, "All right, hop in."

Beck does so, stepping over the runes on the ground and standing awkwardly in the epicenter of the circle. Adam gestures for him to sit; he does, frowning in bemusement. With Adam rushing around lighting candles and sprinkling water along the ground, Beck doesn't know why all he's being told to do is sit right. He feels useless and doesn't like it. Every time he opens his mouth to help, however, Adam just shuts him down with a shake of his head and another firm order to stay inside the circle.

It's not easy to argue with Adam when he's taking charge, so Beck doesn't. The magic Adam is working is fascinating to watch, even if he doesn't understand a bit of it.

The last candle to be lit is a large, heavy, white one. Adam takes a moment to carve sigils into the side before taking a flame to it (and his *hands* again—Beck might have a problem), and once the flame has caught he sets it down in the circle, right in front of Beck. Beck is busy trying to study the inscriptions on the sides when the lights suddenly go off.

Startled, Beck looks up to find Adam stepping back into the circle, a large bowl in his hands. The bowl looks like it's made out of some sort of crystal, but the water in it glimmers like stars in a pitch-black sky. Candlelight enables Beck to see the expression on Adam's face. He looks calm as he ever has, and self-assurance ebbs some of the anxiety gnawing at Beck.

"Here's what we're gonna do," says Adam, kneeling in front of him. "I'll hold this bowl over the candle, and all you have to do is look into the water. Look into the water, let your mind go, and you'll remember."

Beck feels underwhelmed. "That's it?"

"It ain't gonna be magic wands and fireworks, so yeah, that's it." The exasperation in Adam's tone sounds almost fond, and Beck huffs a laugh in spite of himself. "It'll be a vivid memory, and it's gonna feel real. Don't worry. I'll be right here the entire time. I won't let anything happen to you."

The idea of Adam staying with him is more than a relief. "So you'll...wake me up if anything happens?"

"You should come out of it on your own, but if you need me to, of course. I'll wake you up."

There's no time to be nervous about this. He can't wait any longer. Adam's here—nothing can go wrong. He trusts Adam, whether Adam likes that or not, and knows he won't let any harm come to him. He can do this. They've *got* to do this.

Now's the moment he finds out how he died.

"Are you ready?" Adam asks, and Beck nods his head. He's never been more ready in his life.

Adam raises the bowl of water over the candle flame. Immediately, flashes of reflected crystal dance all over the room, filling the circle with light. Beck tries to marvel at them, but his attention is stolen by something else. The flicker of the flame within the water is hypnotizing. Beck finds himself drawn in, leaning further over the bowl as the water in front of him burns.

The light draws him in. It isn't long before it's all he can see, dancing flame filling the darkness in his vision. He couldn't tear his eyes away even if he wanted to, and he's not sure he wants to.

"Good," Adam praises, rich voice making his words drip like honey onto Beck's skin. "Great job, Beck. Focus on that."

Beck focuses, and he tries to let his mind wander in the way Adam told him to. He's not sure it's working until Adam starts to speak again in a low murmur.

"For what you seek,
Your mind holds fast,
Draw you back
Into the past."

The incantation only sticks in Beck's mind the first time. Though he is conscious of Adam repeating it, over and over, it is suddenly impossible to focus on anything. His mind is being consumed by candle flame, and all he can see is its brightness, its flicker, its shadows—

He's caught in a free fall, with nothing to catch him, and no panic to freeze the blood in his veins.

He feels...

Snow.

Snow crunches under Beck's feet, his light sneakers leaving imprints with each step. He's goddamn freezing. Not that he's about to admit it, because he'd die before he gave James the satisfaction of being right ("You go out in those and you're gonna be walking on blocks of ice. They'll have to cut off your damn feet!"), but maybe it wasn't the best idea to wear these shoes today.

He'd thought he and Dylan would be able to run to work—it would be faster than fighting James's ancient

Jeep through streets that haven't even begun to be cleared yet. The lash of ice and wind across his face, however, makes it clear he isn't running anywhere.

"We shoulda just taken the car," Dylan yells over the storm, pulling his parka tighter around his shivering frame. "Why didn't we take the freaking car?"

"We're the ones dumb enough to leave the house," Beck hollers back, though they both know it's not really their fault. Their boss couldn't let them off from work on New Year's Day—with the city being wracked by the biggest snowstorm it's seen in years. Aside from them, the streets are deserted. No one is going to be buying CDs today, but Mr. Eberly had made it very clear that if they didn't come into the shop today, they wouldn't be welcome tomorrow.

Dylan stumbles over the curb and slips. His arms flail, and he almost goes down. For a moment he is pinwheeling, suspended in midair like a building during the split second it implodes.

Beck's arm lashes out at the last instant and seizes his brother before Dylan can land on the icy street. Wide-eyed, Dylan huffs a breath and turns to look at Beck.

"Thanks."

He is pale against the backdrop of white. All his color is washed out—his face looks bloodless, making the dark freckles on his skin stand out with sharp clarity. His eyes, usually a warm chestnut, now seem pitch black, and the shock of messy brown hair upon his head reminds Beck of a sharpie scribbled on blank paper. He looks like a kid again, the same annoying middle schooler who used to hang around Beck's room and bug him while he was trying to get his homework done. Dylan gets on his nerves a lot, but Beck feels a sudden rush of affection for him so strong that it surprises even him.

"*Stay on your feet, Dyl,*" *is all he says, clapping his brother on the shoulder as they both step off the curb. "I ain't haulin' your ass off the street if you decide to slip and—*"

He doesn't see headlights. He doesn't hear a shriek of tires, or a grinding of brakes, because the car isn't stopping. It certainly isn't looking out for two dumb kids crossing in the middle of the road, right in its speeding path.

Dylan is one step ahead of him, and Beck doesn't think before he acts. He throws himself forward, body-slamming Dylan with all the force he can put behind him. Dylan goes skidding across the street, hitting a nearby light pole hard, but he catches himself before he can fall—

Beck feels the impact slam into the left side of his body.

For a moment, there is nothing. There is pain, so blinding that he cannot think. The world seems to explode in a white-hot flash, and everything fades out. There is no sound, no feeling, no life flashing before his eyes. There is only pain.

The first thing he feels, when he remembers how to feel anything, is cold. Iciness is seeping into his skin, and he realizes he's lying in the middle of the street. When he tries to take a breath, he gets a lungful of slush. Beck chokes on it. He opens his eyes. Instinct tries to get him to turn his head from its awkward angle, but he hasn't so much as twitched before a sharp pain in his neck causes him to freeze.

He's facing Dylan. He can see his brother crouched on the safety of the sidewalk. Wide black eyes, depthless pools in a colorless face, staring at him. Dylan's gloved hands twitch. His chest is heaving, but he doesn't move. He stands, frozen, like the rest of the world around him, and watches

Beck. Though Beck tries to focus on his brother, Dylan is blurring away into the white around him.

The next thing he knows, hands are on his face, on his shoulders, and someone is shouting in his ear. Dylan's right next to him now, lifting him off of the snowy street. Beck can feel his head land on Dylan's bony knees, can hear Dylan urging him to "stay with me, dammit, come on…"

None of it feels real. This isn't real.

He can't feel his body, and that's how he knows he is only dreaming. In dreams, you can't feel anything, so that's how you know it isn't real. He can't feel his own injuries, or Dylan's desperate hands. All he feels is the cold seeping into his skin.

When that melts away too, Beck realizes he must be waking up.

"Beck!"

There are hands on his shoulders, shaking him. Beck jolts awake as if he's been underwater and comes up for breath. A desperate gasp fills his lungs with air, and he immediately chokes on it—it feels so wrong to be breathing when he just *felt* the life seeping out of him. Eyes wide, he reels back from Adam and lands hard on his hands. As pain rockets through his wrists, he is dragged back to reality once again.

It was a memory. He died, out there in the snow. He *died*, but now he's alive, and he can remember *everything*.

"Oh God," he gasps. "Oh my God."

"Beck, look at me. What did you see?" Adam says, reaching out to him. He looks as startled as Beck has ever seen him, eyes wide with concern. Beck can't focus on Adam now. He can't escape the memory of the car plowing into him, of his hands on Dylan's back as he pushed him out of the way.

Those same hands now press to his face, a weak barrier between himself and the world. Panting raggedly into his palms, Beck squeezes his eyes shut and fights the overwhelming urge to sob. "A hit-and-run," he moans instead, and laughs out loud. "Oh my God. It was a damn hit-and-run!"

His eyes are stinging. It's hard to breathe past the burning in his throat, and he wishes he had a pillow, either to punch or to hold tight. "I died in Dylan's arms. After pushing him out of the way. Stupid kid wasn't even looking, he didn't see... We didn't... I *died*."

He opens his eyes at last, lifting his face to meet Adam's own. Adam has crawled closer; at the sight of the tears streaming down Beck's face, he visibly recoils.

"I'm dead, Adam," Beck says. "I'm actually dead."

And for the first time since he woke up, everything is *real*.

Chapter Seven

THE PILLOW IS soft beneath his head, pliant no matter how hard he tries to press his face into it.

Maybe if he holds still for long enough, he'll fall asleep. Maybe he'll get lucky and wind up smothering himself into unconsciousness. It is preferable than having to lie awake with his roiling thoughts, fighting to suppress the unease bubbling up every few seconds.

Beck pulls the covers tighter around his body and inhales the rich scent of a body that does not belong to him. Everything in this room smells like Adam, from the tables to the floors, but especially the bed. This is the place Adam sleeps every night, and now Beck is smearing tears all over his pillows. Jesus, he's a mess.

Faced with a semi-hysterical Beck, Adam had found himself at a loss. He didn't know what to do, so his best idea was to bundle Beck up with blankets and tea before imploring him to "get some rest."

There was no reason he had to lead Beck all the way up to his room and let him curl up in his bed, but Beck is more than grateful that he did. If Adam hadn't been so kind, he probably would have wandered off and done something stupid, like gone home a wreck, or called his family—who still have no clue he's back.

(*There's* a conversation that's goin to go over well. *Hey, Mom, don't freak out, it's just your son, back from the dead!* He'd wind up giving his poor mom a freakin' heart attack.)

Instead, Adam parked Beck in his room and gave him some space. It was a gesture Beck couldn't appreciate more if he tried. He's had time to pull himself together (he's failed) and try to gather his thoughts (he doesn't like any of them).

Of course, that doesn't make things any better. He's still dead, and now he can remember every second of his death in vivid, painful detail.

A large part of him wishes he'd never gone through with the spell. Another part is grateful. At least he knows now, no matter how much it hurts him. At least he knows.

(*Knowing* is the problem too. He *knows*.)

The memories resurface once more, as vivid as the first time he lived through them. Beck recalls the feeling of the car slamming into him and can't help whimpering as he hugs himself closer. Of all the ways to die—like, it wasn't as if he'd hoped to go out in a blaze of glory, but *hit by a car*—

And Dylan. Poor, poor Dylan. No wonder the kid wouldn't talk to him. Beck died in his little brother's arms, and he's spent the past few months torturing himself over it. Now Beck is back, and Dylan has no clue how to deal with it.

It explains so much—hell, it explains everything. Beck almost wishes he still had no clue what was going on.

"Beck."

The voice at the door startles him. He jolts up in bed, fighting out of his blanket cocoon. He knows the only person he'll see is Adam, but he isn't about to ignore the guy when he's done so much for him.

(The malicious voice in the back of his mind whispers that Adam is a researcher; of course he'd want to learn more about the kid who came back from the dead. Maybe all Beck is to Adam is an experiment, something to be observed...)

Adam looks hesitant, hovering in the doorway like he doesn't quite know what to do. "Are you...feeling better?"

Beck opens his mouth to speak and lets out an animalistic moan instead.

Oh God, he's a mess. He's a total mess. Unable to look at Adam, he presses his face in his hands as the waterworks start up all over again. He can't face him (or anyone, but especially him) when he's so pathetic.

He hears Adam rush across the room, by Beck's side in an instant. "Easy," he urges, placing a hand on Beck's shoulder. Beck jerks away and immediately regrets it. "Just breathe."

Beck takes a shuddering breath and winds up choking on a sob. He presses a fist to his mouth, humiliated and furious and lost.

"Hey, stop crying. Come on." Adam's hands paw at his face, but Beck twists to keep him from getting too close. He hates falling apart like this. The last thing he wants is for Adam to see what a mess he is. As soon as he catches sight of his blotchy face, tears and snot making his cheeks damp, he'll be disgusted. He'll walk away (and he *should*, because Beck's freakin' *dead*) but God, Beck can't stand the idea of him walking away.

He doesn't want to be alone right now. He doesn't want Adam to leave.

Adam just keeps prodding, no matter how much Beck tries to keep him at a distance. "Beck, come on," he insists, running his thumbs along Beck's cheeks. "Look at me. You're okay. It happened, but you're okay now. You're alive, and everything's gonna be fine."

"You don't know that—" Beck hiccups and bites down on the rest of his words because he sounds pathetic.

"Yes, I do." And of course, Adam sounds assured as ever. "I know that because I know you. Maybe I don't know you well, but I've seen enough that I know you won't stop fighting until everything's back to the way it should be. Because you're that stubborn." Beck gives a wheezy laugh, half a sob. "And you're strong enough that you can do it."

"I can't get my life back," Beck rasps, shaking his head. "I died, it doesn't—it doesn't work like that, I'm *dead*—"

His voice breaks on the last word, ending in a whimper. Beck pulls away from Adam once more and buries his face in his hands.

"That ain't true," Adam says, and he almost sounds angry. "Look at yourself. You're *alive*, Beck. You're the most alive person I know."

"I'm not," Beck insists, but Adam catches his wrists before he can go on. Stunned into silence, Beck doesn't struggle as he is pulled forward and doesn't even protest when his hands are guided away from his face.

Adam takes Beck's chin and guides it upwards, until he has no choice but to meet Adam's eyes. "Look," Adam orders, and Beck has to. "Look at me and tell me if I'm lying. You're going to be okay."

There isn't an ounce of dishonesty, no flicker of uncertainty in his gaze. The confidence Beck finds instead is overwhelming. He opens his mouth, inhaling shakily, and finds that he can't tear his eyes away from Adam's.

The dark pools are steady and warm, filled with a surety Beck only wishes he could feel within himself. He wants to lose himself in them; he wants to immerse himself in that calm and drown.

Adam still has a hold on his wrists; his thumb strokes slowly along Beck's veins, while the hand resting beneath Beck's chin comes up to cup his cheek. Adam's touch is as steady as his eyes, as warm as the breath that escapes through barely parted lips.

"Look at me," Adam says again, and Beck can't look away.

He can't speak, even if he wanted to. Adam finds his voice where Beck's is lost. "You're more alive than anyone I've ever met. You're funny...and stubborn, and determined, and loyal, and unique. I'm amazed by you, Beck."

Beck takes a breath, and hardly feels it fill his lungs. At this point, the air he's breathing is mostly Adam's, and he is close enough to see the flecks of midnight brown in his otherwise black gaze.

"You're alive," Adam whispers, and Beck feels the words against his lips.

When Adam kisses him, he soars. It is a firework show bursting inside his chest; it is the finish line at the end of a race; it is the opening song of a rock concert; it is thrilling, it is electrifying, and it sends life pulsing through Beck's veins. He kisses back with as much force as he can manage, fearful of hurting Adam but terrified of him pulling away.

They move against each other's mouths until they are compelled to part for breath. Beck pulls back, only long enough to gasp against Adam's mouth, before he presses forward once more. Beck's shoulders hit the headboard of Adam's bed, but he doesn't care—nothing else matters when the man on top of him is holding him like he never wants to let go.

"Adam," he whispers. "Oh God—"

Just as suddenly as it began, Adam jerks away, out of Beck's grip. Stunned, Beck struggles to grapple with his empty hands and burning lips. He feels naked without Adam against him. As he sits back up, brow furrowing in confusion, he finds Adam struggling to his feet.

Beck's jaw drops in surprise and dismay. "Wait! Sorry—do you not like people who say 'Oh God' while kissing? Does it weird you out? I didn't know you were religious—I could never, ever do that again—"

Adam scrambles backwards, away from the bed and away from Beck. He is wide-eyed. For some reason he looks horrified, and Beck has no clue why.

"I'm sorry," Adam spits out. "That was—inappropriate. That was wrong, I should never have done that—"

"Adam, hey!" Beck tries reaching out, but Adam stumbles backwards towards the door. He can feel his heart sink, a heavy rock weighing down his stomach. Does Adam not like men after all? Or does he just not like Beck? Did he do something wrong?

"I gotta—I gotta go," Adam says, and he looks so upset that it twists Beck's heart. "I'm sorry, Beck."

He sprints out of the room, slamming his door behind him. A few seconds later, Beck hears the apartment door shut as well.

He collapses back against the pillows, a moan tearing from his throat before he can stop it. This is what whiplash feels like. Stunned and confused, Beck struggles to comprehend why Adam acted like he'd hurt him as he rushed away. The only rational explanation is that Beck must have done something wrong—but *what*?

Hell if he's going to let Adam get away without an answer. One of the things you learn coming back from the dead is how stupid it is to waste time instead of acting. Beck refuses to let Adam run away from him.

He sprints out of the apartment and double-times it down the stairs, only to find Adam's shop empty. He isn't sure what he expected, but the counter unmanned and the bookstore deserted isn't it. With no sign of Adam, Beck backtracks, shutting the door behind him and turning back to the hallway.

Like the first time he ever saw it, the same image of old TV game shows flash into his head. There are three doors; behind one is the person Beck is searching for. If he picks the wrong one, he might not find Adam, and if he picks the right one—

What will happen then?

He can't overthink it. Beck lunges towards Door Number Three and finds Adam in his magic room, sitting in the middle of the same circle he drew for Beck hours ago.

"Adam," he gasps, and the other man starts. Adam begins to rise to his feet, but Beck is already moving towards him. Before he can escape, Beck catches his shoulders and holds him tight, forcing him to look at him.

"Why'd you run away?"

He's never seen Adam look this uncomfortable. He is shamefaced, unable to meet Beck's eyes, and he squirms as if he's only just restraining himself from yanking out of Beck's grasp. "What did you want me to do, Beck?" he demands. "I kissed you."

"Yeah...you did." Beck tries to bring a hand up to the side of Adam's face, but he turns away. "And I gotta admit, Adam, I've wanted that to happen more than once, but that wasn't how I imagined it would go."

"I shouldn't have done it. You're upset, you're crying, and I just...took advantage."

"You didn't!" The absurdity of the statement makes an incredulous laugh bubble up Beck's throat. "Not at all! Adam, it's okay."

"It isn't."

"I wanted—" Adam looks up at him sharply, as if only registering Beck's confession of a minute ago. Beck takes a steadying breath before he continues. "I wanted to kiss you. I wanted you to kiss me. I didn't...didn't think it would happen."

Adam huffs incredulously. "Why not?"

"I...didn't think you liked me."

"Beck, you think I'd let someone drag their friends into my house at three in the morning if I didn't like 'em?" Now Adam's the one who looks amazed, in an indignant sort of way that suits him a lot better than his earlier shame. "Or do a spell for someone I don't care about?"

"You did a spell for me," Beck agrees, and finds himself nodding. "You did. Because you...care about me?"

By the look Adam gives him, it should have been obvious.

Slowly, they sink to the ground. Adam is still in Beck's arms, only now he isn't pulling away. He's pressing closer, allowing Beck to run a hand through his hair, brushing his fingers over the smooth curve of his jaw. Adam's skin is warm, and Beck is enchanted by the smoothness he feels under his touch. "Tell me why you did the spell for me, Adam," Beck says softly, and Adam's eyes flutter shut.

"I've got magic in my blood," he explains, voice a low murmur that Beck has to lean in even closer to hear. "I grew up in New Orleans, in the French Quarter, where magic's just another part of life to most folks. My grandmother was a priestess. She'd been practicing the old traditions since she was a little girl, knew more about them than anyone. She could summon, curse, heal... She was the most powerful witch I ever saw. My grandfather was an exorcist by trade. When my papa grew up, he followed in his footsteps." Adam takes a deep breath, leaning into Beck's hold. One of his fingers is tracing a gentle pattern on the back of Beck's shoulder.

"Papa was killed by a demon when I was ten. Maman was left to take care of three kids, and Grand-mère helped some, but we all had to fend for ourselves. We all found our own ways—with or without magic. One of my sisters became a witch; the other decided she wanted nothin' to do with magic. And me, I left New Orleans behind. I got rid of the accent, and got rid of the person I used to me. I ran away.

"After I left, I swore off magic—didn't want any part of it in my life. I wanted to get as far from it as I could, so I moved to a small city, where I hoped I wouldn't find any. But you don't choose it, it chooses you, and by the time I opened up this shop I knew more about the hidden worlds than anyone else you could find around here. When the Tresser Corporation tracked me down, they gave me cash in exchange for helping 'em with whatever they need to know. And...they need to know a lot. So that's what I became—a librarian of sorts. But not a witch. Never real magic."

He bites his lip, and when he raises his head again, he looks frightened. "Until you, Beck. I don't know why it's different for you, but it is. I care about you more than I've cared about anybody in a long time."

"I—why?"

"I don't know," Adam says, and laughs. "You're...alive. You're so alive, and not even dying could change that. I can't help wanting to be close to you."

Adam's hand comes up to cover Beck's. "I feel like you're changing my mind," he whispers, "and it's terrifying, but I don't want it to stop."

Beck can't breathe. Adam is close, so close that he can feel his words murmured against his skin, and the last thing he wants to do is pull away. If Adam's really spent the whole of his life being afraid of what magic can take from him, then what does Beck represent—what magic can give?

If that's what he is to Adam...he's okay with that.

"Adam," he murmurs, and when Adam tilts his head up, Beck kisses him again. It's shorter than the last—slow, gentle, a tender press of lips. Beck doesn't push, and when they both pull away, Adam looks awestruck.

"Now I know you," Beck whispers, "and you know me. That's a pretty good start, huh?"

"I want to know you more," Adam spits out, impulsively, and then looks surprised at himself. Beck—more than experienced with his mouth running away from him—can't help the grin that breaks across his face.

"Me too," he admits, and Adam's eyes warm until they look close to melting. "Why don't we? We can go out together—learn more about each other—not move so fast—"

"But we don't have to move slow," Adam hastens to add, and Beck giggles.

"No, not slow. Just fast enough."

Adam looks up at him, dark eyes twinkling with something that Beck could almost swear is magic. He looks happier than Beck has ever seen him, warmth spreading across his face like dawn breaking over a morning sky. Beck can feel the same warmth spread within him, drowning out the turmoil of earlier and replacing it with something warm and self-assured. He can't remember the last time he felt this happy in his life.

His life. He was alive, and he died. Then he came back to life. All of this is true, and it's okay, because Beck is alive *now.*

He is alive, and he has never been more certain of that than with Adam's lips pressed against his. With Adam in his arms, Beck's heart feels ready to burst out of his chest, and he's never felt this way in either of his lives. It's thrilling. It's exhilarating. It's hopeful.

It's *a new start*, and that's what Beck needs. Instead of putting the pieces of his old life back together, Beck needs to start fresh. A brand-new slate—after all, how often do people get to come back from the dead?

He'll call his parents. He'll reenroll in school. He'll fix things with Dylan. He'll have Adam too, which is more than he could have expected.

If this is his new life, Beck is glad Adam is here to help him begin it.

Chapter Eight

HE STARTS BY making phone calls.

Beck's cell phone is dead, so while it charges Adam is kind enough to let him use the phone in the corner of the bookshop. Beck sits at a table, on the phone with his university directors as he tries to inquire about picking up where he left off. He doesn't outright say *"I came back from the dead"*; in turn, the woman on the phone doesn't inform him that it's not possible to reenroll with all his credits intact.

As he navigates the channels of this tricky conversation, Beck watches Adam at work. At his usual place behind the counter, Adam is meticulous. He sorts through the store's records, takes stock of the cash register, and greets every customer who comes in with a polite smile. Adam's attachment to his shop is obvious. He knows every book, every title, and gladly helps people find what they're looking for.

It's fascinating to watch Adam in his element. More than once, Beck finds himself distracted from his phone call. Adam smiles down at a book in a particular way, or huffs to himself as he reshelves something, or mutters under his breath, and it's just... Well, he'd have better luck focusing in the middle of Cirque du Soleil.

"Sir," the woman on the phone prompts after the third time Beck trails off in the middle of a sentence. "I can't answer your question if I don't understand it."

"Right. Sorry." He forces himself to snap back to attention. He's been going in circles over this topic long enough that his brain feels fried. He's starting to wonder if it would be easier to not go back to school at all. "If someone who's been through three years of college drops out, then reregisters—umm, where would they be, tuition-wise?

"Did the student have any scholarships?"

"Uhh, ha-ha...yeah, no." A familiar chime rings through the shop (a ward, Adam explained earlier, signaling someone is about to enter), and Beck forces himself not to look up. "No, nothing like that—uhh, sorry, I mean, they were already a junior—"

"Oh. Hey," Adam says. "I was callin' you before."

Beck frowns down at his papers in frustration. Trying to make sense of the information he's scribbled down is like solving a thousand-piece-puzzle when all the pieces are the same color.

"I know," a familiar accented voice replies. "I got your messages."

Startled, Beck looks up. He recognizes Sophie in an instant. She stands with her back to him, approaching the counter and Adam in slow, heavy steps. Her blue dress looks wrinkled. Her dark hair is loose, hanging in her face, and the pocketbook slung over her shoulder looks heavy enough to bludgeon somebody with.

A sharp pain shoots through Beck's head, and the pen he's holding slips from his fingers. He comes close to dropping the phone, too, but manages to remain steady. His first thought is that something must have happened over the other end of the line; suddenly there is a screech of static in his ears, and his head feels blurry.

It takes him a second to realize that it isn't the phone at all. It's *him*.

He manages a small groan as he slumps forward, hand coming up to cradle his pulsing skull. The voice over the phone line goes ignored. Slowly, he brings the phone down to rest on the receiver once more. Out of the corner of his gaze, he sees Sophie take another step closer to Adam, and a stone drops into his stomach.

"Hey, are you okay? You don't look good." Adam's voice is heavy with concern. He takes a step out from behind the counter, even closer to Sophie. Beck wants to scream at him to stop, but once again finds himself paralyzed.

"Sophie—" Adam cuts himself off. His silence speaks more than any exclamation of horror could. Sophie lifts her head, hair falling away from her face, and Beck already knows Adam is seeing bottomless darkness in place of her eyes.

(*He's been here before. This has happened before. He's seen this beforebeforebeforebefore—*)

"Get out of her!" Adam snarls, voice dipping low in a rage so fierce that it sends a jolt down Beck's spine. It feels like a lightning strike—Beck's nerves are electrified for a single second, but it's enough to break the spell that rendered him helpless. He lurches to his feet, a shout already tearing from his throat, as the possessed Sophie pulls her hand from her pocketbook.

A large, silver knife gleams in her grip. She lunges.

"*Adam!*"

Adam staggers backwards, nearly tripping over his own feet. He regains his balance just in time to dodge the knife that comes swinging towards his head. As he flees behind the counter once more, Sophie is hot on his trail; the blade in her hands is a shining omen of death. Beck's legs can't carry him fast enough. He sprints across the shop, but before he can reach them, Adam darts into the hallway, and the door slams shut behind him.

Sophie is quick to follow, but Beck grabs her before she can get the door open all the way. He gives no thought to his own safety until he sees the knife slash towards him. A sharp pain in his cheek tells him Sophie has found her target. When another shout tears from his throat, Beck tastes blood.

He wraps both arms around Sophie and tries to force her to the ground, but she fights back hard. When she throws herself back, Beck is slammed into the counter. The wind is knocked out of him just long enough for Sophie to land another blow to his ribs and worm out of his grip. She's tearing into the hallway before Beck is able to pull himself back up.

His head is still screaming. He feels dizzy, nausea trying to force its way up his throat. The idea of staying down settles over him like a gentle blanket, and Beck is shocked by how tantalizing it is. He could do nothing; he could stay still, close his eyes, and *listen*—

Another shout from the backroom snaps him out of his haze. Beck's eyes shoot wide open. *Adam.*

What is he doing? How could he think of not helping when Adam is in danger? What's *wrong* with him?

Beck struggles to his feet, panting past the ache in his ribs. Hot liquid drips down his face; when he lifts a hand to his cheek, it comes away stained red. Baring his teeth, he shakes his head in disgust and charges into the hallway.

The doorway leading to Adam's apartment is wide open, and Beck can see feet kicking at the top of the stairs. His only thought as he rushes forward is that he prays he won't find Adam bleeding, with a knife jammed somewhere it shouldn't be. The thought of Adam hurt terrifies him even more than the voice in his head still hissing at him to hold still, and he throws himself at the first body he sees—the one clad in blue and wielding a knife.

He probably should have considered the whole *stairs* thing first. The thought doesn't actually occur to him until they're *both* tumbling down, Beck's arms locked around the possessed woman's body. Sophie grunts under him, letting out an animalistic screech as they fall, only to be cut off by the ground's impact.

There is no time to recover. Beck rolls on top of Sophie, pinning her to the ground. She still has her arms free, and her knife swings up to catch his jaw. He only misses it by twisting his body to the side. The blade catches solid air, and Beck catches her arm before she can try again. Before he can get to the other, however, her free hand seizes his hair and yanks, hard.

"Ow, dammit!"

He slams her body into the ground with enough force that her eyes (once gray as the winter ocean, and now pitch black) go wide. Over his shoulder, Adam shouts something; Beck can't hear it, he can't think of anything except the knife still clutched in her hand—

She yanks her arm out of his grip with a surge of strength he was not expecting. Her fist slams into his jaw, knocking stars into Beck's vision.

In the second it takes Beck to recover, time seems to slow down. He sees Sophie's knuckles, white around the gleaming hilt of her knife. He sees her hand descend in a wide arc, headed straight for his back. He sees the flash of bloodlust in her eyes, in the jagged twist of her lips, carrying the certainty that her attack will not miss.

He rolls off of her just in time to avoid the knife about to plunge into his back. Instead, it buries itself deep in Sophie's stomach.

"Sophie!" Adam's anguished holler makes his presence known. Beck hears the clatter of something hitting the ground and footsteps pounding behind him. He catches Adam just before he can throw himself at Sophie's side, hooking his arms around his waist and holding him back. Sophie's eyes are still pitch black, staring up at the ceiling in their own twisted victory. As much as Beck wants to look away, Adam's agony is even harder to face.

The man in his arms is cursing him, writhing and fighting with all his strength. He wants to be let go; he wants to rush to Sophie's side, but Beck knows he can't. Though he tries to hush Adam, his words are drowned out by Adam's own panic.

Amidst the chaos of Adam's struggles, Beck almost doesn't see the cloud of black smoke stream past Sophie's parted lips and dissipate into thin air.

For a second, he can't comprehend it. Then Sophie lets out a choked, agonized whimper, and Beck knows.

He releases Adam so suddenly that he loses his balance, hands and knees hitting the ground hard. In the next second Adam is scrambling to Sophie's side.

Sophie is flat on her back, both hands pressed over the wound in her stomach. Her eyes—gray as a steel blade—are wide and glazed with pain. She stares up at the ceiling. Each gasp for breath causes her to jerk, lips moving soundlessly.

Adam throws himself into action without wasting a second. The knife in Sophie's abdomen has become dislodged, allowing a startling amount of blood to bubble up from the wound with each breath she strains to take. Adam presses his hands down, heedless to the crimson staining his hands. There is a manic determination in his eyes that steals Beck's breath. He is determined to hold the life in his friend's body by any means necessary.

On the ground, Sophie still forces breath after desperate breath into her lungs. She twitches with each gasp, a dying bird struggling to get off the ground. *"Je meurs... Je meurs..."*

Adam grits his teeth at the whimpered words, bending his head to his work. *"Je suis désolé,"* he mutters; though Beck can't understand the words, he hears the raw agony within them. *"Je suis vraiment désolé..."*

Half delirious from pain, Sophie's eyes land on him. A flicker of relief crosses her face at the sight of a friend. *"Adam? Qu- Qu'est-il arrivé? Comment—"*

She cuts herself off with a sharp gasp, face screwing up in agony. Blood bubbles between Adam's fingers. As Sophie trembles in pain, convulsing beneath Adam's hands, he struggles to hold it all in. Her very life is seeping from her body, running across the floors and staining her dress a garish crimson. There is too much bleeding for Adam to control. He can't stop it, no matter how hard he tries, no matter how desperate he is. His friend is slipping away, and he can do nothing but watch.

That doesn't mean he's going to stop trying. When his hands aren't enough, he hastily pulls his shirt from his own body and balls it up before pressing it against the wound. "Sophie," he says, leaning close. Beck can hear the tremors in his voice as he struggles to sound reassuring. *"Réspire. C'est d'accord. Tu vas bien."*

"Ça fait trop mal..."

"Je sais. C'est d'accord." Tears stream down Adam's face, glistening trails along his dark skin. He stubbornly blinks them away, focusing on his work. His chest is heaving as he fights to control each breath, and his knuckles are white around the shirt in his hands. *"Désolé..."* he whispers again, and in a smaller voice, "Sorry... I'm so sorry..."

"Adam..." Sophie's hand twitches. She makes an attempt to lift it, but strength has deserted her. *"S'il te plaît..."*

Adam doesn't divert from his work, but his face twists in agony. "Beck," he grunts out, and it takes Beck's horrified mind a moment to realize he's being addressed. "Hold her hand."

Wide-eyed, Beck can't process the request. Adam tears his focus from Sophie's wound for one second, just long enough to send Beck a fierce glare. "Get over here and hold her hand!"

Startled into action, Beck scrambles over to grip Sophie's straining hand. Her skin is cold already, damp with her own blood. For a second he has to fight not to pull away; instead, he squeezes, and Sophie squeezes back.

Not knowing how to help and unable to do anything else, Beck can only look into Sophie's feverish eyes. He doesn't know what to say. Saying nothing feels cowardly somehow, as if he's hiding from reality by not trying to help her. He would, if he only knew how. How does one comfort someone who's dying in front of them? Beck doesn't have a clue. He hopes his expression can reassure her, as much as she can be reassured, but wishes he could say something.

When he was dying, Beck remembers, he didn't realize what was happening. It felt like a dream. He closed his eyes, and it all faded away, like the last note of a song, or a movie screen fading to black...

"It stops hurting," he whispers, leaning in close enough for Sophie to hear his soft words. "Once that happens, it's as easy as falling asleep."

"Beck, shut up!" Adam snaps, something tortured in his voice. "She's not dying."

But there is a flicker in Sophie's eyes—not quite understanding, but relief—and Beck knows he said the right thing.

"I can't—*dammit*, I can't stop the bleeding," Adam hisses through his teeth, pressing down hard enough to make Sophie's body tense. Her grip on Beck's hand tightens, then goes slack all at once. For one horrible second Beck is sure she's died, but then Sophie pulls out of his grip. With one last burst of energy, she places her hands over Adam's.

Adam's frenzied motions cease. He goes completely still.

Tears stream down his face, just as they slip from the corners of Sophie's eyes. An entire silent conversation passes between their locked gazes, incomprehensible to anyone else. At last, haltingly, Adam draws his hands away from Sophie's abdomen, bringing her hands with him.

"I'm gonna stop this," he whispers. "I'm gonna keep this from happening again."

Sophie huffs out a breathless giggle, spots of blood flecking her lips. "You'll finally take my advice?"

"Best advice I've ever gotten." Adam nods, a sob cutting off his last word. With no small amount of effort, he forces it back down. "I'm not going to be afraid anymore."

"You can... make something beautiful, Adam," Sophie whispers. "Use it to help. That's who you're meant to be."

"I wish I could help you," Adam whispers, and presses his forehead to hers. The dying woman's eyes flutter shut; for a long moment they stay that way, their hands clasped tightly and their brows touching.

Beck sees the moment Sophie's face relaxes—the moment her grip on Adam's hands goes slack. Adam doesn't pull away for another moment, and when he finally does he is trembling.

Carefully, he takes Sophie's hands and lays them upon her chest. Then he sits back from the body, draws his legs up, and hides his face in his knees.

Beck tries to reach out, but something stops him. It is a sudden chill coursing down his spine; the sensation of eyes on his back; the sudden certainty that they are not alone.

He turns and comes face-to-face with a shadow of a different kind. The figure of Alyssa at the end of the hallway startles him. Dressed all in black, with her hair wild about her face and her clothes dark, she looks more like an angel of death than a human being. She is standing still, not moving an inch, even when she notices Beck's eyes on her.

The girl lifts her head, revealing wide eyes in a tear-streaked face. She looks traumatized; her thin frame trembles like a leaf caught in a windstorm.

"H-hey," says Beck, slowly rising to his feet. Alyssa takes a step back, stumbling, as she shakes her head.

"It wasn't supposed to happen," she says.

"What? What wasn't?"

Beck's head is pulsing again, an ache that is becoming too familiar to him. As he watches, Alyssa raises a hand to her own head and exhales a whimper.

"They keep saying it should be this way. But it shouldn't. This isn't supposed to happen!"

(*It is. This is how it should be.*)

"Who?" Beck demands, voice pitching in fear. "Who's saying that?"

"Them," Alyssa replies, gripping her head in both hands. "I didn't mean to hurt her, I didn't! I couldn't stop it! *They're* the ones, not me, but I can hear them—they're in my *head*—"

"Who?" Beck's own head is screaming as loud as Alyssa's shrill cries. Maybe he's yelling too—he's not sure. "Who are they?"

"They've been here before," Alyssa says, and Beck's eyes go wide.

(*He's been here many times before.*)

He never got headaches before he died. Only since he came back to life have these spikes of pain become commonplace.

(*This is the way it should be.*)

They're in his head too. They have been, all this time. They were there with James, they were there with Sophie—

They're here now.

(*We've always been here.*)

Alyssa falls to her knees, sobbing, and Beck clutches his own head as an icy vice settles around his chest. Memories of his headache while talking to James in the kitchen emerge; of the pool attack, and the screaming in his head; of the skull-splitting pain when Sophie entered the shop. The Tresser Corps agents' words echo in his head, and he feels sick to his stomach.

He tried to convince himself that he came back the same person he died as—that he brought nothing with him whatsoever. He was wrong.

He is dangerous after all.

Chapter Nine

"HOLY SHIT" IS the first thing James says when he walks into the shop. "What the hell happened here?"

Beck rounds on him, fury in his eyes. It's not fair, but he can't help it. Adam's holding silent vigil over Sophie's body in the magic room. Alyssa's catatonic up in Adam's apartment. Beck called his friend here because there's a crisis, and James's mouth isn't what he needs right now. They have to figure out what to do. "What d'you think happened? I text you that someone's dead, then someone's freaking dead!"

"Hey!" James obviously sees how freaked out Beck is; after a few seconds, his temper simmers back down, and he holds up his hands as the shop door closes behind him. "Calm down. Get your head screwed back on, and tell me what happened. The others are on their way now. We'll figure out what's going on and deal with it."

"We can't," Beck mutters, grabbing a fistful of his hair and pulling. "She's dead."

"Who?"

"Sophie!"

"Great! You wanna tell me who Sophie is?"

When he opens his mouth, Beck finds himself unable to answer. Instead, he turns on his heel and walks down the hallway, knowing James will follow. His footsteps are steady until he reaches the end of the hall. A red stain mars the hardwood floor, and James mutters a curse under his breath. Instead of lingering, Beck pushes open the door to the magic room.

No light is on, but the room is still illuminated. Candlelight flickers against the walls, casting heavy shadows over everything. He can't force himself to cross the threshold. The sight of Adam, kneeling beside a circle of candles with his head pressed to his folded hands, is enough to constrict Beck's heart.

Sophie's hands are carefully folded across her stomach, covering up the ugly wound that dyed the fabric of her light dress crimson. The ring of candles surrounding her makes her skin look waxy. Firelight dances over her placid face, casting her long lashes into shadow and lending color to her bloodless lips.

"Oh," James says, after a long moment of observing the morbid scene with his mouth agape. "Cookie girl. Right."

The recognition is so inappropriately-timed that Beck can't help a hysterical laugh. Once he's started, he feels certain that he will never stop...but the sound dies in his throat, and it seems just as certain that he will never laugh again.

ADAM DOESN'T BREAK, and that's the worst part. Even once Sophie's makeshift altar has been extinguished and he has shut the door to the dark room behind him, he remains stubbornly stone-faced. When Beck tries to ask him if he's okay, he brushes him off.

"I'm fine, Beck," he says. "We've got more to worry about now."

Something in Beck's brain stirs when he says that. It is an electronic hum, like picking up on a radio frequency that's just static. His hand flies to his head, but Adam doesn't see. His back is already to Beck, and he walks past the stain on the ground without looking down.

Now that Beck is conscious of the things in his head, he can't stop hearing them. It is a constant drone at the back of his skull, every so often growing too loud to ignore. When its pitch rises, it hurts. Sometimes the pain is blinding, and sometimes it's just a dull thrum that he can push out of his mind, but it is always there. It's been there since the moment he woke up, and so have they.

(*We've been here before.*)

He doesn't know what they are. He doesn't know why he can hear them. The one thing he knows, in the deepest depths of his being, is that they are wicked, and if he allows them to raise their voices, something terrible will happen.

Adam would probably have a clue. He needs to tell Adam, but there's no way he can when he's still in mourning over his friend. The catatonic girl upstairs is enough to deal with. Beck refuses to put this burden on Adam's shoulders too.

Alyssa hasn't stopped crying since Sophie's death. She keeps gripping her head, muttering to herself in a voice too soft to be understood. She won't look at anyone, even Adam. She won't speak to them, and she refuses to allow herself to be touched.

Adam is obviously at a loss. Alyssa was Sophie's friend. They were college roommates, he explains, and in that time grew to be close. Alyssa died of meningitis—it was sudden, jarring, and Sophie was still reeling from her death when she suddenly reappeared outside Sophie's apartment door. At first, Alyssa's case had presented just like Beck's; she was sick, confused, and had no idea she was dead. Sophie was the one to take her back into what used to be her home.

"She was so worried," Adam mutters, frowning at the curled-up figure of Alyssa from the doorway of his bedroom. "Kept saying she wasn't adjusting well... She was having nightmares, then not sleeping at all. Kept getting bad headaches. Sophie didn't know what to make of it." He swallows hard, and a crack appears in his stony expression. "She kept saying it was like she wasn't back at all."

Beck considers this, and wonders if it's been the same way for his friends. He doesn't think he's been behaving any differently. Maybe he's been a bit sullen, more thoughtful, but he's had reasons. Adjusting has been a challenge, and it's disorienting to think he *used* to be dead—

His mind flashes back to his breakdown in Adam's room. Is it possible that was just this afternoon? If he hadn't snapped back to normal—if Adam hadn't pulled him out of the current intent on sweeping him out to sea—would he have wound up like Alyssa?

Eventually, they manage to coerce Alyssa out of Adam's bed, only for her to plant herself in the middle of Adam's couch. James—sitting at the end of the couch and staring at Alyssa like he's witnessing the zombie apocalypse—not-at-all-subtly inches away.

Adam coaxes her into accepting one of his sleeping potions, but while it sedates her it does little to endear her to talk. Even Beck's appeal, out of earshot of the other two, that he "can hear them too," gets him nothing more than a sideways glance and a sniffle.

When the rest of the group finally arrives, Dana dragging a reluctant-looking Dylan behind her, they all convene in Adam's living room. Instead of centering around Alyssa, they focus on Beck and Adam as they take turns telling the story of Sophie's possession.

"There was...no way to save her," Adam admits, after Beck recounts Sophie's last moments. "I had the stuff for an exorcism, but I wasn't fast enough... That demon had its claws in her and was out to kill. If it didn't kill her, it wouldn't have stopped till we were both dead."

Beck remembers those two hollow pits of blackness in place of familiar eyes—James's, and then Sophie's. A shiver courses down his spine; the pulse in his head grows a bit more intense. He grits his teeth to block it out, focusing instead on the horrified reaction of his friends.

"It's not safe," Dana says, frowning down at her clenched fists. "This is all a goddamn nightmare."

"What can we do?" James asks. "You've gotta give us somethin', man. If the world's going nuts, I need to know how to fight back."

"Adam doesn't do exorcisms," Beck says immediately. He knows how uncomfortable Adam is with magic and isn't about to force him to teach his friends. "Cassandra said she'd help us, so if we call her—"

"I'll do it."

Beck cuts himself off, turning towards Adam in surprise. The other man's jaw is set. His eyes are downcast, but there isn't a flicker of uncertainty on his face. He looks dead-set on his decision, and when he lifts his head to regard the group once more, his assurance is clear. "I can teach you a bit of demonology and go over the basics of an exorcism. I'll give you the stuff you'll need."

As Beck gapes at him, Adam's eyes flicker towards him. It only lasts for a second, but it is enough for Beck to realize that he knows what he's doing—or, at least, he's sure he does. Whether Adam will regret breaking his own rules or not, nothing is going to sway him now.

"It's the least I can do," he adds. "I made a promise, and I'm gonna carry it through."

Beck's friends look visibly relieved at that. The stiff set of Dylan's shoulders relax, while Dana's fingernails stop digging into her knees. James runs a hand over his face before his attention is drawn back to Alyssa, curled up in a ball at the other end of the couch.

"And, uhh—what about her?" he asks, pointing with his thumb. Adam's attention flickers back to Alyssa as well, a deep frown settling on his face.

She still hasn't said anything. Now she's looking at them all with wary eyes, her face drawn with exhaustion. When everyone's attention turns to her, she shrinks back, curling further into the arm of the couch.

"Alyssa?" Adam asks quietly. "I know... I know it's tough, but can you tell us what happened to Sophie?"

Alyssa's lips part, and for a moment it looks like she's ready to speak. Then, just as suddenly, she shuts down again. It's like a door slamming in their faces. Adam deflates, while Beck presses a hand to his forehead. For a moment, he was sure they were getting somewhere.

Then Alyssa raises a hand, her finger extended—in Beck's direction.

"*He* knows," she accuses, voice a tear-roughened rasp. "He hears them too."

Just like that, Beck is the one in the spotlight, and he gapes under the sudden weight of the room's attention. Inquiring eyes fix on him. He falters, not sure what to say, before swallowing hard and clearing his throat.

Adam has one eyebrow raised in silent question. It churns Beck's stomach; he does know what Alyssa is talking about, but he doesn't know how to explain his awful revelation.

What if he loses what he has? Once they realize the truth—how horribly wrong he is—they won't trust him. They'll realize he isn't whole, isn't the Beck who left them, and they'll be terrified of him. Adam will turn his back. They'll all desert him, and they *should*, because something dangerous is inside him.

Beck can't let that happen. He can take the risk. He can't be abandoned by the only people he has.

"I don't know," he says, giving a quick shrug. "I have no clue what she's talking about."

For the most part, this answer is accepted. Alyssa isn't making a great case as the paragon of mental stability. It's easy to write off her feverish ramblings as just that, and even though Beck knows it's wrong, relief surges through him when the attention turns off of him.

The only one who doesn't stop staring is Adam. His eyes still pierce Beck, inquisitive, and with a hint of suspicion that Beck can't ignore. Desperate to soothe Adam, he gives a small smile. Adam's shoulders relax just slightly, his eyes turning away, and Beck exhales in relief.

He just can't afford to lose what little he has right now. If he has to keep this darkness to himself—and maybe that's the safest thing for everyone—then so be it.

He can live with that, for a little while.

THE BASIC ANATOMY of an exorcism is simple. There are two steps: to subdue, and to expel.

Many different tactics are associated with exorcisms, across various religions and societies. None of these are less effective than any other, but Adam teaches the group the most commonly used practices—not to mention, the most simple. He goes over the necessity of getting a demon immobilized, then shows them the sigils used to expel them. Each one is a complicated twist of lines and shapes, nice to look at but frustrating to draw.

Afterwards, Adam passes out sheets filled with a basic exorcism incantation (in Latin—Beck's brain feels ready to explode) and explains that this should cast the demon out and banish them back to Hell. There is no known way of killing a demon.

He also passes out various supplies that he explains might prove useful—from bottles filled with cleansing water, to pure rock salt. Sage is handed out, and Adam shows the group how to smudge it.

Everyone takes to the instruction with different degrees of skill, but they all match each other in enthusiasm. James and Dana are a bit too enthusiastic—they nearly knock over a bookshelf while shouting incantations at each other. When he drops his sage, Beck comes close to setting the room on fire (no one is surprised). Most unexpected is Dylan, who attends to the instructions with frightening focus. When he reads off the Latin, Adam praises his diction. His sigils are scribbled, but precise.

Really, Beck isn't sure why he's surprised. Dylan has always been a whizz kid, and a quick learner. He's a scholarship student; ever since high school, he's worked his tail off to keep up his grades. Beck just never expected his brother would be such a natural demon hunter.

"You all should be set," Adam announces a few hours later, once everyone has tucked their borrowed supplies away. "You ever run into a demon, they won't know what hit 'em."

Clapping each other on the back, the group files up to Adam's apartment once more. Adam is the only one who trails behind, hesitating in the doorway and closing his eyes like he's thinking hard about something. Beck watches his brows furrow, shoulders slumping, and wonders if he should say anything.

He's never been good at keeping his mouth shut. "Adam?" he ventures, voice low beneath the herd of footsteps stomping up the stairs. "Are you okay?"

"I just..." Adam trails off, worrying at his lip, before heaving a sigh that shakes his entire body. "I feel like there's a piece missing. There's gotta be something I'm not seeing, a reason why this is happening... I just don't know what it is." Beck tenses. Adam, busy running a hand through his hair, doesn't notice. "I know there's something causing all this. I've just gotta find out what."

If anyone can figure it out, Beck thinks, it would be Adam. The thought makes him feel sick.

IT'S CONVENIENCE THAT finds everyone crashing at Adam's house that night. Alyssa won't leave Adam's house; Adam won't leave Alyssa; Beck doesn't want to leave Adam; and James refuses to let anyone leave, seeing as it's past midnight and "if demonic shit is running around, something's gonna happen at night. Something always happens at night."

Alyssa retreated back into Adam's room before the exorcism lesson, and they find her sound asleep in bed when they return. Adam just sighs, and with Beck's help hauls a few extra pillows and blankets out of the closet. They're given permission to sleep where they like. James and Dana wind up twined together on the couch, a mess of limbs, making it hard to tell where one body ends and the other begins. They murmur to each other in the darkness, every so often laughing softly. On the floor, Beck stares wide-eyed up at the ceiling, cringing anytime he hears what sounds like a kiss from above. It's impossible to block them out. The only one who has any sort of luck is Dylan, who buries himself in a blanket cocoon and pulls a pillow over his head to protect himself from the inappropriate PDA.

Adam is somewhere downstairs. Beck doesn't know where, but he's learned by now that Adam rarely sleeps when he's supposed to (in fact, he's not sure he sleeps at *all*). Unsure of where Adam might be, his mind runs rampant. He imagines Adam bent beside Sophie's body, tending to her throughout the night. Or perhaps Adam is hunched at his counter, pouring over pages of notes on demons and possessions, trying to find the missing piece to tie the entire puzzle together (the knowledge that Beck has, and doesn't dare say out loud).

How can he tell Adam the truth? He doesn't know; he doesn't think he can. He focuses instead on sleep, and tries to force himself to get there, but the more he tries to ignore one thing, the harder it is to block out another.

The whispering is getting louder. He can't escape it. When he presses a pillow over his head, it is only amplified by the silence. When he tries thinking of something else, the spikes of pain in his head intensify until his brain is locked in a haze of pain.

By the time he can't take it anymore, he is grinding his teeth against the ache. It feels like drills being pushed into his head. The static is starting to overpower even the sound of James's snoring, and he wants nothing more than to tear his hair out.

Tossing and turning does nothing to help. Even sitting up and cradling his head in his hands brings him no relief. Beck needs the world's biggest aspirin—that, or to open his skull and take out his brain.

After a few minutes, it's impossible for him to sit still anymore. He rises to his feet, careful not to disturb any of the sleeping bodies around him, and stumbles towards the door.

He takes the staircase slowly, clutching to the railing in the dark. He does not know the stairs well enough to recognize the creaky spots in the wood. Each sound feels like a siren blaring through the building, announcing his break for freedom: *The prisoner is escaping! Code red! Close cell block 23!*

Once he's finally back on the ground floor, he breathes a sigh of relief. Then he realizes exactly where his feet have taken him. His heart seizes up in his chest. He's standing right in the spot where Sophie died.

When Beck looks down, he's able to make out a dark spot staining the wood beneath his feet. His stomach lurches. He clamps a hand over his mouth to stifle a moan and reels away from the spot.

He finds Adam exactly where he expected to. The door to the back room is ajar; candlelight still flickers across the walls and ceilings, and Sophie's body lies in the center of the room in her makeshift altar, just as Beck remembers it. Adam, however, is hunched in a different area of the room, pouring over a spread of papers. His glasses are sliding off the bridge of his nose, but he does not seem to notice. His brows are deeply furrowed. His chest heaves with shallow, manic breaths, and his eyes dart back and forth across the page as if searching for a secret code hidden in the mass of notes.

Every instinct in his body urges Beck against interrupting, but he cannot leave Adam—not like this.

"Adam?" he says softly. "Are you...okay?"

Adam looks up for a brief second, as if startled. Then his face clouds over again, and he returns to his work. It feels like a door slamming in Beck's face. "I'm fine, Beck," Adam mutters. "I'm okay. I have to work on this. I have... I have to understand."

Adam is anything *but* okay. Beck simply does not know a way to help. He is not sure if he should, or even can. The last thing he wants to do is leave Adam, but instinct tells him there is no way to help him like this, now.

(Except telling him. He could tell Adam everything, the thoughts, the whispers—but that would tear down every bit of the tentative haven he has built. Beck cannot lose everything. He cannot lose himself.)

"Okay," he says. "Please get some rest soon."

He closes the door behind him.

He refuses to let Adam's candlelit visage haunt him on his way up the stairs. There is nothing else he can do, he tells himself. Adam is mourning. He needs to find answers on his own.

As for Beck, he just needs...sleep. Peace. Sanity. All things that seem impossibly elusive to him right now. (A wicked, half-human voice in the back of his mind whispers that they never existed at all.)

He does not want to return to bed, he decides once he reaches the top of the stairs. He needs a glass of water first.

The apartment is dark; Beck finds his way by shadow, hands held in front of him to keep him from walking into anything. By the time he reaches the kitchen, he feels dizzy from pain. He's so distracted that he almost doesn't notice the shadowed figure hunched at the counter until it suddenly shifts.

"Geez!" he hisses, stumbling back and crashing into the wall. "What the hell?"

The figure rises to his feet. "What are you doing?" demands a familiar voice.

"Dylan? What are you sitting in the dark for?"

"What are you walkin' around here for?" Dylan counters, drawing himself up to his full height. It's not impressive; even standing on his toes, he's still shorter than Beck. (Conscious of his own unimpressive height, Beck pities his brother. Genetics are a cruel mistress.) When Beck starts fumbling along the wall for a light switch, Dylan snaps at him to knock it off. "You wanna wake everybody up?"

"No. Sorry." That's the last thing Beck wants. Reluctantly, he shuffles around in the dark in search of the sink.

For a few seconds, Dylan remains quiet. He allows Beck to walk into the fridge, trip over a chair, a throw rug, and his own feet before finally asking, "What are you looking for?"

"The sink. I just want water."

"God, here. You're useless."

"Thanks, Dyl," Beck mutters as he feels a cold glass being pressed into his hands. It occurs to him that Dylan had this sitting on the counter, but the glass remains full. Whatever drew him from sleep, it wasn't a need for water.

He takes a sip of the cooling liquid and finds it does little to soothe the ache in his head. Only then does he dare to venture, "So, why're you up?"

Dylan's at the counter again, back turned to him. "Can't sleep. It isn't weird for me."

It was before Beck died. Then again, it's obvious by now that so much has changed that Beck doesn't even know where to begin. Even so, he has a good idea what the cause of this particular change could be.

There's a large part of him that doesn't want to say a thing. It's not the time; it's not the place. Dylan won't want to talk about it even if Beck does broach the topic, and he knows there's a strong chance of this ending in a shouting match. Still, he can't remain silent, not with the memory of Dylan cradling his dying body still fresh in his mind.

He understands why everyone was so eager to keep the truth from him; they didn't want it to change him, the way it changed Dylan. It haunts him now, and he's only just remembered it. Dylan's been *living* with it for seven months.

Beck cannot escape the burden of responsibility on his shoulders. Dylan's suffering is his fault. He doesn't regret saving his brother's life for a second, but he regrets leaving him alone.

So even though the words stick in his throat, Beck forces himself to push past it. "Dylan...look, I remember, okay? I didn't, but...I do now. I know what happened."

Dylan's shoulders go stiff. He doesn't turn around. "What's it matter, Beck?" he says after a moment.

"It matters because I died in your arms!" It's too early to lose his temper, and it's not fair, but Dylan sounds so *dismissive* that he can't help it. "It changed you. I can see it, and I can't stand knowing I was the reason why. I'm back now, and you can't forget what happened, but we can move on—"

A glass slams down on the counter, nearly hard enough to break it. Dylan's still form is wrought with tension; he's almost trembling with it.

"Move on," he says.

"We've gotta try. I'm back, and much as you don't like it, if we don't keep going with our li—"

Dylan lurches around and forward, hands outstretched. The kitchen table rattles when he hits it, and he shoves the nearest chair out of the way. Suddenly he's just inches from Beck's face. "Move on?" he demands, voice a low growl. "You think I can *move on* just 'cause you're back now? You think you being here makes things better instead of worse, huh?" His teeth bare in a humorless grin. "When did you become so damn selfish?"

Something inside of Beck jerks, like a match struck but too stubborn to catch. "What the hell'd you say to me?"

"I said you're goddamn *selfish*."

Dylan lets his words hang in the air between them. The only sound is their breathing, each chest heaving with agitated pants. When Dylan speaks again, his tone cuts like a razor. "You didn't think, Beck; you just did. I was in the way of that car, not you. It should have hit me, but you shoved me away. It shouldn't have been *you*, but you died anyway, and I had to live with that. Did you think about Mom and Dad? About me? About all of us? No, not for a goddamn second!"

"Our family can survive without me!" Beck spits back, feeling his temper flare. "You know Mom's got nobody else except you, so don't act like what I did—"

"How much do you think we've all been mourning over you?" Dylan demands. "Do you think we took you dying *fine*? Do you think we've just moved on, like you were nothing? You haven't even called them, Beck! How does your family feel?"

"I don't know," Beck retorts.

"Mom cried for a week straight. She couldn't even stand up at your funeral. Dad started drinking again. Uncle Cliff had a heart attack. Molly waits at the door every day just crying, because she doesn't know when her owner's gonna come home. They've got your picture all over the house. Now all Mom does is sit at home looking at our baby albums and watching those old videos of us as kids. She doesn't even *cry* anymore."

Every word hits Beck like a bullet to the chest. He recoils, even as his brother takes another step forward. "Did you know any of that? Did you?"

"I didn't know!" Beck spits back, fire lacing his tone. "I didn't know, because nobody tells me goddamn anything!"

"Maybe that's 'cause *you're not supposed to be here*!"

This is all he can take. Beck snaps. He lashes out, shoving Dylan with enough force to make the smaller man reel back. He catches himself against the kitchen counter, hands swinging up to steady himself. Beck's vision is red. He can feel each breath entering his lungs, labored and furious; his skull is roaring, his heart is pounding, and the realization that he's come this close to hitting his own brother infuriates him more. What the hell is Dylan's problem? How dare he accuse Beck of being in the wrong here, like he *asked* to die, like he *asked* to come back? "I saved your life! You can't just be grateful, you've gotta be a brat about it! Like always, Dylan, right? Like your entire life!"

"Don't act like you know who I am now!" Dylan hollers back. "You've been gone for seven goddamn months! A lot's changed, Beck!"

"Don't you think I know that?"

"*Maybe you don't!*"

Beck's head is screaming. He's screaming. *Everything* is screaming. "If it weren't for me, you wouldn't be alive!"

Dylan lunges forward, aimless and desperate. "Well, hell," he shouts back, words amplifying in Beck's head like he's hollering them over a loudspeaker. "Maybe I'd rather have died than be the one who had to deal with *killing you!*"

Suddenly, Beck's vision explodes. The pain in his head goes from agonizing to blinding; the static turns into a shriek; alarms sound, storms rage, and his knees hit the ground hard as he can no longer remain standing. A strangled moan tears from his throat, hands flying to his head.

It hurts, dear God, it *hurts*, he can't *stand it*.

(*We've been here before. This is how it must be. This is the only way.*)

No, thinks Beck, and that's all he can think—all he is able to think, all he has time to think—because a single noise cuts through the cacophony of chaos and pain. It is a sound Beck has heard a dozen times before, in a dozen different circumstances, but none as awful as this.

He hears Dylan gasp.

Beck forces his head up just in time to see a shadow— swirling, writhing, pulsing with tiny flashes of electricity— force its way through Dylan's open mouth.

His brother slumps forward. For one awful moment, he is motionless as a marionette with its strings cut. Then he jerks. His arms sway, his neck twitches, and he exhales in one massive breath.

Beck's lungs have turned to stone. He can taste his heart in his throat. Even before Dylan lifts his head, he knows exactly what he will see.

Dylan's eyes have always been a warm brown—filled with all the *life* intrinsically tied into everything that he is.

When Dylan lifts his head, his eyes are pitch black.

Chapter Ten

"DYLAN," BECK EXCLAIMS. Another moan is drawn from him as the pain in his head spikes once more. Dylan steps forward, feet heavy on the tiled floor. His breathing echoes through the dim kitchen, until he is right above Beck.

Dylan crouches down until he is level with Beck. Dark hair hangs in his face as he peers down, lips pulled back in a blood-curdling sneer. His skin looks washed out in the shadowed light, making the emptiness of his gaze all the more prominent.

"You thought you could save him," Dylan—or the thing that is inside Dylan, but is *not him*—says. A low laugh crackles from his throat. "How sweet."

When he stands up, it is sudden. Beck doesn't realize he's no longer looking into Dylan's face until a foot catches him square across the mouth.

He sprawls across the floor, reeling from the blow; he tastes blood.

"Humans do such things for each other because they are naive," the demon says in Dylan's voice. "They are the most selfish species, but they so ardently try to deny their own nature. They are vicious, then kind. They kill a man, then show him sympathy. They stab, and then bandage the wound they inflict. Humans are a futile species simply because they cannot accept their own natures."

Beck tries to pull himself from the floor, but the pain racketing through his head leaves him slumping back down with a groan. The demon laughs again, like gravel running through a compressor.

"You're fighting spirit is charming. You care for this human. He is your friend."

"Don't hurt him," Beck grinds out, spitting blood onto the floor. "*Don't.*"

"Why have I taken his body?" asks the demon; his tone implies the answer should be obvious. "Do I want to have a conversation? No! If I had my way, I would go into the next room, kill every breathing flesh sack there. I would go downstairs and do the same. Then, I would plunge this knife..." Deliberately, he pulls a steak knife from the block on the counter; it glints in the faint moonlight. "Into this body's heart. I will feel the lifeblood seep out of him, wait to the last breath...and take his soul down. That is the goal of We, the Righteous Legion. Destruction of the human race, at any cost. I am a soldier, fighting for the superiority of my species, and any human or demon who dares stand in the way will feel the wrath of the Righteous upon their heads."

Great, Beck thinks. He's gotten his brother possessed by a member of the demonic Übermensch.

"I can't do that," finishes the demon. "I won't have the time, or the chance. I only have the time to bring down one tonight, and it will not be you. You are far too great an asset, Deathwalker."

Beck hears the sound of the kitchen drawer opening, and the clink of metal rings through the air. Panic surges up his throat, forcing him to struggle once again. His mind flashes with visions of Sophie's blade. Sure enough, when he looks up, Dylan has a large steak knife clasped in his hand.

"How fitting," the demon says, a smile cut from glass playing on Dylan's young face, "that the downfall of the humans will come at the hands of their own dearly departed."

Beck *needs* to get up. He needs to push himself to his feet and wrestle the knife from his brother's grip, but once again Beck is paralyzed. It is not the desire to stay still that now immobilizes him; it is the utter inability to do anything. He tries to force his limbs to move, but they have turned to stone. His veins are filled with lead. He is tied down, frozen, powerless. All he can do is watch his brother be forced to kill himself.

(*This is the way it's supposed to be.*)

No! He died saving Dylan. He has to be able to save him now. Beck screams out in his own head, trying to force himself to move, but he is helpless. Dylan raises the knife; it glints in the dim light.

"You have been a great asset to us, Deathwalker."

The knife swings towards Dylan's chest.

"*Not so fast*!"

Dylan goes down at the hands of a linebacker tackle, and it's the greatest thing Beck has ever seen. The demon does not have the chance to react; James is on top of him, pinning him to the ground, before he can realize what hit him. James lunges for the knife and manages to wrestle it from Dylan's grip. Spitting, swearing, he tosses it aside and keeps Dylan down.

Dylan is half James's size, but he is possessed by an unnatural strength—whether it is supernatural or desperation, Beck has no clue, but he thrashes in the grip of his restrainer. Unholy howls tear from his throat, curses and condemnations mixed with venomous taunts.

"Shut the hell up," James snarls, smacking Dylan hard across the head. Stunned, the demon falls silent for a second, which is all the time James needs. "*Dana!*"

As if on cue, the lights flick on, and the spell is broken. Suddenly Beck can move again, he can breathe, and he can think past the screaming in his head. As he scrambles to his feet, he catches sight of Alyssa, wide-eyed as she watches from the living room, but she is blocked by Dana charging forward, crumpled piece of paper in hand, wielding a sharpie like a sword.

"Hurry up, come on," James urges, swearing as Dylan lashes out at the sight of the newcomer. Unintimidated, Dana hits her knees at her possessed friend's side and yanks up his shirt to reveal the bare expanse of Dylan's scrawny chest. She doesn't hesitate for a second before she begins to sketch out the sigil.

Dylan's howls grow louder, as if every stroke of the pen burns him. It's killing Beck to see him in so much pain; instead of getting in the way, however, he helps to pin Dylan's legs down. Satisfied with her work, Dana rises and stands over the chaos, peering down at her paper.

"*Impius spiritus,*" she recites, "*exorcizamus te, in nomine Domini et beatus mundi! Et abierunt! Cessa decipere humanas et revertatur ad te mundi diaspora—*"

"Diabolica!" James hollers over the sound of Dylan's shrieking. "It's diabolica!"

"Fuckin' diabolica then, do I look like I speak Latin?" Dana hollers back; then, eyes narrowing in focus, she finishes. "*Diabolica! Hic non receperint vos! Ut mittatur foras, te rogamus, audi nos!*"

A rush of black smoke bursts from Dylan's mouth in a deafening scream, tearing like severed nerves from a ravaged throat. His back arches in his friends' iron grips; veins bulge from his forehead, bloodless face twisting in an expression of agony. Beck's ears fill with a roar that drowns out the rest of the world.

And just like that, it's over.

The sudden hush of silence that falls over the room is such a relief that Beck could cry. Dylan—the *real* Dylan—looks very small as he slumps back, limp as a ragdoll, into James's arms. James immediately cradles him to his chest like a child, and hovers over his unmoving body. One hand cups Dylan's cheek; the other gently rubs his back. When James looks up, his face is pale, and Beck feels his stomach drop.

A tense second passes before Beck notices Dylan's chest rise and fall. His mouth is partially open; a tiny wheeze escapes him. "It's okay," James gasps, sounding choked. "He's all right, just passed out."

"Oh thank God," moans Dana, burying her head in her hands as she slumps forward. Beck huffs a half-hysterical laugh.

It only takes a minute for Dylan to revive. His head stirs against James's chest. A groan slips past cracked, bleeding lips.

When he opens his eyes—bruised, shadowed, but clear and perfectly human—he squints up at the group around him. "What the hell happened?"

Beck can't help it. Throwing himself past everyone—even James, who he's sure will fight him for a first look at Dylan—he throws his arms around his baby brother's neck.

For a long moment, Dylan is tense. He doesn't move; he doesn't even seem to breathe. Beck squeezes even tighter, clutching Dylan as if he never wants to let go.

Finally, Dylan's arms come up, and he hugs Beck back.

The rush of euphoria is almost overwhelming. At once, any residual trace of the fury of earlier melts away. Beck pulls back, conscious of the tears running down his face, and finds Dylan in the same state. This is who Beck died for the first time, and he would do it all again.

"I'm sorry," he says, but Dylan only shakes his head.

"No, man, you—you've got nothing to be sorry for. It's me—"

He cuts himself off, inhaling a shaky breath, and the two embrace again.

There's no reason to say any more. They both understand. The wounds they tore in each other's skin knit themselves back together with a whisper. In a single second, seven months of hurt is healed, and Beck whimpers even harder as he feels the weight melt off his back.

Their friends give them a moment before they butt in—which they do, of course. "What's with the waterworks?" Dana finally interjects, throwing her arms around Beck and Dylan at the same time. "Come on, kids, it's okay."

"Yeah. Quit actin' like something bad happened," James says, but he's grinning as he pulls the small cluster into a hug. "Everything's peachy. We handled this. We can take on anything now."

Allowing himself to be engulfed by the warmth of his friends—his *family*—Beck feels a sense of wholeness that he'd been missing since he woke up. With Dylan returned to them again, it truly feels like things are back to normal.

Of course, they aren't. A spike of pain in his head reminds him of this, and Beck wiggles out from the dogpile as his face clouds over. The last thing he wants to do is hurt his friends—but he has, and the knowledge of that isn't something he can bear again.

He turns and comes face-to-face with Adam.

Standing in the doorway, Adam observes the chaos with a look of measured focus that Beck has become familiar with. His eyes scan the knife on the floor, the discarded sharpie, the chaos of overturned chairs and crumpled rugs. They turn to the tangle of friends on the ground. Finally, they land on Beck.

Adam has been here the whole time, Beck realizes. He stood back, watching, as the rest of the group handled the exorcism—but he's been here. He saw, and he heard.

"Adam," he says, realizing that he no longer has anything to hide.

Very slowly, Adam turns to look at Beck. There is a new light in his eyes, a spark of victory that renders Beck speechless. "I got it," he says. His voice is low, but not with anger; he sounds victorious. "I figured out the answer."

"WAIT, OKAY—SO what are you saying?"

Sighing, Adam slumps forward. One pointed finger slams repeatedly against the counter, as if he's praying to shatter either marble or bone. Beck can't blame him for his exasperation, but he also can't blame his friends for asking the same questions that are swirling through his head. Adam's explained this three times, and it still doesn't seem real. "I'm saying the only way to get here from the demon world, besides being summoned, is through an opening. That could be anything that breaks the demon-human barrier—a tear, a weak spot, an open door. What I'm saying is, Beck and Alyssa are open doors."

Dylan's face is squished against his palm, fingers twisting in dark hair. His struggle to process this is obvious. James just looks constipated, biting down on his lower lip so hard that Beck's amazed he doesn't chomp it off. Dana looks ready to walk away from the conversation entirely.

As for Beck, he's feeling every emotion at once. Relief that Adam has finally figured out what's going on is mingled with horror. He's the one who's been hurting his friends the entire time—he didn't mean to, but that's what happened. As great as it is to know what's happening to him, he almost wishes his friends didn't. At least then he wouldn't have to worry about them fearing him.

In the chair next to him, Alyssa shifts. Her bony shoulders knock against Beck; she casts him a wary look and inches away. He offers a smile he hopes she'll find reassuring but knows the skittish girl must be having an even harder time dealing with this than he is.

(After all, he might have gotten two friends possessed, but he saved them both. Alyssa and Sophie were not that lucky.)

"What they're doing is basically channeling demons—like a medium can channel spirits. The demons are using their energy to get into the human world, and that's how they're possessing people. It's not their fault, and *they're* not possessed themselves—they're letting the demons through without even meaning to." Adam leans across the counter, staring at the two no-longer-deceased individuals intently. "Isn't that right?"

Beck is the first to nod. Next to him, he sees Alyssa bob her own head, hiding behind a curtain of dark hair.

"I also," Adam continues, after he is met with a round of stunned silence, "think I've figured out when possessions happen."

"Oh really?" Dana crooks a dark eyebrow, looking torn between being impressed and worried. "When's that?"

Beck already has a clue, but hearing Adam put it into words validates everything he's been feeling all along. "Possessions are triggered by someone feeling strong emotions. Joy, sadness, anger. Any of this stuff in extremes can open a window for a demon to come through."

When James got possessed, he'd just finished telling Beck how happy he was to have him back. Sophie was upset with Alyssa. He and Dylan were in the middle of an argument. Chaos led to even more chaos, and created the perfect opportunity to let something awful in.

The realization makes something in Beck curdle. This means he can't be around people anymore. He got his own brother possessed, for crissakes. If he can't keep from channeling demons, how's he supposed to go on living? How can he ever hope to reconnect with his family, his friends again, if he can't control this wicked thing inside him?

As if reading his mind, Adam meets his eyes. His lips twitch—a quick, almost imperceptible movement, but it floods Beck with a sense of calm he didn't realize he needed. "Thankfully," he says, sounding perfectly pleased with himself, "I've got a plan for fixing this mess."

"Okay," Dana says, "and what's that?"

Adam smiles before turning to Beck and Alyssa. "How would you two feel about a job?"

Epilogue

THE DOOR OF the bookstore slams shut, rattling the walls. Heavy footsteps echo throughout the shop like a stampede of buffalo. The intruder stops in the middle of the shop, looks around, and bares his teeth in frustration.

"Beck!" James booms. "The hell is taking so long, huh?"

Beck jolts, nearly falling backwards. He regains his balance just in time to keep from hitting the floor. Leaning back, his messy head emerges from around the doorframe of a closet as he peers across the room at James. "Sorry!" he calls. "Just gimme a minute, I'm coming!"

James rolls his eyes and slumps against the counter, shaking his head. From her position manning the register, Alyssa doesn't hide a small, amused grin. She's been smiling more and more these days, and every unashamed show of emotion from her thrills Beck and Adam. She is, slowly but surely, settling back into herself.

"Why am I not surprised?" James huffs. "You've been stuck here for a week, and now when it's finally time to leave you don't *want* to—"

"Will you shut up? I'm coming!" Beck hollers, disappearing back behind the bookshelf once more. There's a grin on his lips as he turns back to Adam, who finally deems it safe to loosen his arms from around his shoulders now that Beck is no longer in danger of falling.

"He's an idiot," Beck mutters. Adam nods before leaning up and pressing another kiss to his lips.

There are a million reasons why they shouldn't be taking a moment for themselves right here, right now—but, well, that hasn't stopped them all week. Beck melts into Adam's embrace, moving his lips against Adam's like a drowning man desperate for a last breath of air. Adam's mouth tastes rich and pleasant. Beck has become familiar with the feel of him over the last week, every limb and every scar, every tiny little perfection.

When they finally pull back, Beck knows his face is red. Adam grins at him. "Better not get too flustered, Beck. Jimmy's gonna think you're excited to see him."

Beck snorts, quickly pecking Adam's lips once more. He can't help himself; pressed up against him like this, Adam is just too much to resist.

Even so, Adam is the one who finally breaks the spell, placing a hand on Beck's cheek to keep him from leaning forward again. His dark eyes are warm as they stare up at Beck, with a lingering edge of pensiveness that Beck cannot ignore. Once again, Beck feels a whisper of that creeping insecurity that has been plaguing him ever since last night, when Adam announced it would be safe for him to go home.

Adam took both Beck and Alyssa in over a week ago, determined to train them to control the darkness which threatened to overpower them. "Every open door can be closed," he explained. His goal was to teach them to do just that.

The next few days had been an endless rush of lessons and mental exercises, meditation and energy work. Beck's never been so Zen in his life. As someone who experiences everything externally, a sudden turn inward was a shock to all his systems. It was bizarre, but over time Beck learned how to acclimate—with Adam's help.

Now, he's almost become an expert at blocking out the whispers. Adam's endless patience saw him staying up with Beck well past midnight every night this week. Together, they practiced blocking out negative energy. Adam taught Beck to anchor himself; he showed him that his mind is stronger than any outside influences.

"Find something you care about to hold on to, and cling to it. Let it remind you of who you are," he told him. "As long as you do that, nothing can overpower you."

(Beck wishes he could say he chose Adam, because that would be romantic as anything. He didn't. Instead, his anchor is the memory of his mom's out-of-this-world beefsteak. Nothing drags him back to himself faster.)

Now, Beck's head is completely free of pain, and any time he feels a subtle spike he is able to push it away. He feels unburdened—especially with Adam pressed up against him.

That doesn't mean the idea of leaving isn't intimidating. Adam was the perfect person to teach him control, because he's so good at remaining levelheaded. Beck has only seen Adam really lose his cool one time, and that's when Sophie died. He's a master at not allowing his emotions to run away with him, so around him it's been easy not to get overwhelmed.

Thrust back into the world of his friends again—with volatile James, emotional Dana, and temperamental Dylan—Beck isn't sure how he'll hold up. He can't help but feel anxious; the memories of those awful nights plagued by possessions flood back to him, and all of Adam's tricks at blocking out negativity can't allow him to forget them.

As usual, Adam can tell what he's thinking before Beck realizes it himself. He runs his thumb across Beck's cheek, brushing the freckles there, and a tiny smile tugs at the corners of his lips.

"You're ready," he tells him—and it's not much, but somehow those two simple words contain every emotion that Adam isn't willing to voice. It's reassurance, confidence, everything Beck needs to hear.

Beck grins back at Adam, and they finally pull away.

Together they emerge from the closet. James's eyes bug out when he sees them, and a groan tears from his throat. "Jesus, that's where you've been? In the shop?"

"I've found them in worse places," Alyssa remarks, and James slaps a hand to his forehead.

"All right, you animal. Ready to come home?"

Beck exchanges a glance with Adam and reminds himself that this is far from the end. He still has a job at Adam's place, working alongside Alyssa. (Adam has made the decision to expand his business; in the past week, more than one magical visitor has walked into the shop and left with an abundance of supplies from Adam's back room. If Adam is going to keep up with supply and demand, he says, he'll be needing extra help.) Alyssa still isn't quite ready to return to the world, and Beck...

Well, Beck is just happy to spend time with Adam every day. He'll seize every chance he can get.

As for college, James promises to get that squared away. If anyone can reenroll a dead man in his classes, Beck has no doubt his indomitable best friend will be able to pull it off.

Then, of course, there's Beck's family.

Beck isn't ready quite yet to return to his parents. He's hurt them. He knows how much damage his death has done, and the last thing he wants is to cause any of them more pain. He's going to return to them when he knows he's ready—and when he does, he'll have his friends (and maybe even Adam) by his side.

Until then, he has his other family. He has James, Dana, Dylan, Adam, and even Alyssa. Looking outside the window now, he can see the rest of the group waiting inside James's rundown Jeep. Dana is idling behind the driver's wheel, and Dylan hangs halfway out the window. When he sees Beck, he waves like an idiot and shouts something Beck is unable to hear.

He's part of something bigger than himself now. The Rogue Always Vigilant Exorcist Squad (*RAVES*, as Dylan was eager to christen it) has been pursuing their goal even in the time Beck has been away. Since their formation, they've tracked down two other ex-deceased people, performed four exorcisms, and prevented countless others from being attacked by delivering the not-dead person to Adam. In his capable hands, Beck and Alyssa aren't the only ones taking back control of their new life...and Lehexe's bookshop has gained plenty of new staff. With Beck joining the group at last, Dana bragged that she is sure they'll be even more efficient.

Putting his life back together won't be as easy as coming back from the dead. There's still a lot Beck has to figure out, a lot he has to deal with, and a lot of baggage to shoulder. Not to mention the whole demon thing, which he's not sure will ever completely go away.

Still, he is determined to make it happen. He's alive; his friends know his secret and are staying by his side; and he's discovered a whole new world. He's found Adam.

All of this is more than Beck can ask for, and it came as a shock to realize he's happier now than he was before he died. His life has gotten ten times more exciting, and he has just about everything he could ask for.

He's alive, and he's happy.

Turning to Adam, he meets his boyfriend's shining gaze and finds himself smiling. Adam's hand slips in his own and gives it a quick squeeze before pulling away once more, and Beck feels energized.

There's no looking back. There's no point in being afraid anymore. Beck is facing the future head-on. As long as he's alive, the only way to go is forward.

"Yeah," he says, turning back to his friend. "Let's go home."

HIS FEET CRUNCH against gravel as he makes his way down the street. Long shadows trail behind him, cast by the bright light of the street. As he passes beneath each street lamp, it flickers and dies.

Taking human form on earth is strange. Appearing human in this world is completely different from settling in the demonic realm. Everything feels heavier here. It feels more real, more intense, as if they are truly a step away from victory. The burden of responsibility weighs upon his shoulders. He draws himself up beneath it, standing tall. He is here on a mission; he has his orders, a job to do, and men to lead.

He knows why he's here.

"Sergeant Valac," he says over his shoulder to the handful of privates clustered behind him. "Is this where we're supposed to be?"

Valac doesn't hesitate. "Yes, sir," he answers. "This is where it all started."

He smiles.

Unit X is exactly where they're supposed to be, and now that they're here, Naberos, Knight of the Ninth Quadrant, knows the real task has only just begun. The Demoniac Alliance has finally arrived in the human world, here to eliminate the threat posed to humans by the invading Righteous Legion, once and for all.

Naberos straightens his collar and steps out into the light of the street. His human legs are steady beneath him.

It's time to get to work.

About the Author

Emilie Lucadamo has too many stories, and not enough words to tell them. At eighteen years old, she has been writing for most of her life, and telling stories even longer. Her dream is to one day become a critically acclaimed author. When not writing, she's probably reading, or spending quality time with her dog.

Twitter: @EmilieLucadamo

Website: www.emiliesbooks.tumblr.com

Other books by this author

How We Sell Our Souls

Coming Soon from Emilie Lucadamo

Where the Night Reigns

In the Darkness, Book Three

The officer behind the desk still looks impassive, if not a little irritated. "We don't have sufficient evidence to consider her missing."

"It's been a lot more than twenty-four hours," Tresser says, narrowing his eyes. "No contact with family or friends, no cell phone activity, no previous indication that she was leaving—" He pauses, raising an eyebrow at the missing woman's frustrated boyfriend, who nods with fervor. Tresser continues, "You've got *every* reason to consider her missing. Why are you sleeping on this? You people are supposed to be the police."

The officer narrows her dark eyes. "We're doing our jobs, sir."

"No," Tresser shoots back, "you're not."

This is not Nathan's battle, but he is impressed by Tresser's strong reaction. He takes a step back, watching as Tresser continues to rant. "The police should be doing what they're paid to do, and instead you're letting a woman's disappearance go uninvestigated for a month while her fiancé is losing his mind worrying about her? What kind of sham are you running?"

"Thank you," the aggrieved boyfriend jumps in, clapping Tresser on the chest before rounding back on the desk. "Now, I'm telling you, okay? My name's Henry Lee. My fiancée's name is Lucy—she's been missing for almost a month now—why aren't you writing any of this down?"

"Sir." Now that the aggrieved fiancé has won more people to his side, he's starting to attract attention from the rest of the station. The policewoman's demeanor switches from bored to serious in an instant. "You're going to have to leave now."

Energized by the support, however, Henry isn't about to be cowed. He slams his hands down on the countertop, creating a bang that echoes throughout the entire station. "I'm not going anywhere until you help me find my wife!"

As his shout dies down, Nathan realizes that every eye in the station is on them. Only once this dawns on him does he realize that they are all pitch black.

Oh, he thinks, *we're doing this now.*

His attention spins back to the policewoman at the counter once more, who is now staring Henry down; her eyes have gone pitch black, ink swirling in depthless wells to exude pure malevolence. Tendrils of shadow writhe in the room's dark corners. The air has grown musky and thick. Tresser stumbles, overwhelmed by the sudden oppressive atmosphere. One hand claps across his chest, the other reaching for the hilt of his gun.

"What the hell," breathes Henry, suddenly very, very quiet.

Tresser is already pulling his gun out of his pocket when he turns to Nathan and freezes.

There is no fear in Nathan's expression; there is no surprise.

"All right," he says, and sounds almost pleased. "That's what I was waiting for."

Also Available from NineStar Press

Connect with NineStar Press

Website: NineStarPress.com

Facebook: NineStarPress

Facebook Reader Group: NineStarNiche

Twitter: @ninestarpress

Tumblr: NineStarPress